THE DEATH SWING AT

Falcon Lake

ALSO BY JEREMY JOHN

*Robert's Hill (or The Time I Pooped My Snowsuit)
and Other Christmas Stories*

*The Strange Grave of Mikey Dunbar and Other Stories
to Make You Poop Your Pants*

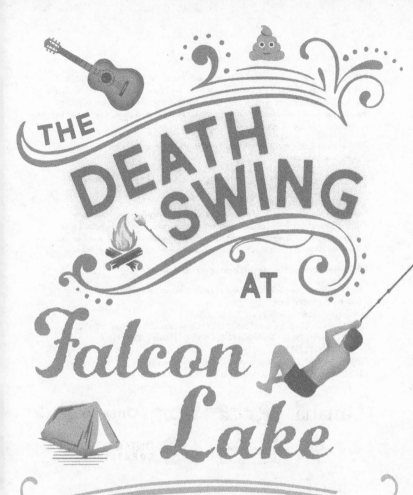

THE DEATH SWING AT

Falcon Lake

and S'more Summer Stories to Make You Poop Your Pants

 JEREMY JOHN

DUNDURN
PRESS

Publisher: Meghan Macdonald | Acquiring editor: Chris Houston | Editor: Allister Thompson
Cover designer: Laura Boyle
Cover and interior images: rope swing: istock/4x6; tent: freepik/moonshinestudio; fish: vecteezy/Mulzz Walet; Guitar: Stockio/Last-Dino; campfire: shutterstock/Lidiia Koval; statue: 58pic; frog: abby-design; Knight: ismail terrab; Basketball: macrovector; Spiderweb: Yevhenii Dubinko; Outhouse: istock/ Creative_Outlet; Wolger: pngitem

Library and Archives Canada Cataloguing in Publication

Title: The death swing at Falcon Lake : and s'more summer stories to make you poop your pants / Jeremy John.
Names: John, Jeremy, author.
Identifiers: Canadiana (print) 2024029954X | Canadiana (ebook) 20240299574 | ISBN 9781459754157 (softcover) | ISBN 9781459754164 (PDF) | ISBN 9781459754171 (EPUB)
Subjects: LCGFT: Humorous fiction. | LCGFT: Short stories.
Classification: LCC PS8619.O4445 D43 2024 | DDC C813/.6—dc23

 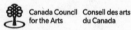

We acknowledge the support of the Canada Council for the Arts and the Ontario Arts Council for our publishing program. We also acknowledge the financial support of the Government of Ontario, through the Ontario Book Publishing Tax Credit and Ontario Creates, and the Government of Canada.

Care has been taken to trace the ownership of copyright material used in this book. The author and the publisher welcome any information enabling them to rectify any references or credits in subsequent editions.

The publisher is not responsible for websites or their content unless they are owned by the publisher.

Printed and bound in Canada.

Dundurn Press
1382 Queen Street East
Toronto, Ontario, Canada M4L 1C9
dundurn.com, @dundurnpress

These stories are dedicated to Manitoba, Canada, (yes, that is a hint about the real Falcon Lake) and the wonderful people there. I moved my family there for my career, and each of us fell in love with our adopted home.

A special gratitude is reserved for my wife. Our time in Manitoba is a perfect example of the sacrifice, dedication, and love that she brings to our marriage. Thank you for everything you are.

CONTENTS

THE DEATH SWING AT FALCON LAKE

IT IS THE PERFECT NAME: the Death Swing at Falcon Lake. It might have been the most perfectly named thing in the whole world. The Death Swing at Falcon Lake. Lots of people had already died, there were lots of ways that the Death Swing could kill you, and it was a swing located at Falcon Lake.

Okay. That last part is obvious. The Death Swing at Falcon Lake was located at Falcon Lake, which was where my family would spend a month each summer at our cottage. We had been doing it for generations. The lake is pretty isolated; there's really nothing else around. The nearest "town" is almost an hour away, and that's really just a bunch of buildings clustered around a single traffic light. Families own all the cottages on the lake, and most have been passed down within those families, some going back more than a hundred years. There's no public access, so no tourists, and there's an informal agreement amongst the owners not to rent out their cottages to strangers. The people of Falcon Lake like it just the way it is. They didn't want it flooded by annoying people from those annoying apps.

The swing part is obvious too. Not a playground swing. You probably gathered that from the "death" part of the name. I doubt there are many pieces of playground equipment with the words "death" in the name. There is nothing called "the monkey bars of death," but if there was, it would be a fascinating story.

This swing is a classic rope swing over a lake: a long, thick length of rope, like the ones used for tug-of-war, with a giant knot at the bottom end. The top was tied to an old oak that grew horizontally from the top of a huge cliff. The oak had most likely fallen during a storm a couple of lifetimes ago. But after the storm ended, the tree continued to grow, so it was deeply rooted in the top of the cliff despite the fact that most of the tree projected out over the water, a huge height above the surface of Falcon Lake.

The top of the rope was tied to a huge branch that stuck out of the oak at a ninety-degree angle. It was the only big branch on the tree. Since it stuck out parallel to the cliff face, it meant that the rope would naturally swing straight back toward the cliff each time. It was as if this one branch had grown specifically so that a rope could be attached. It was the perfect branch, on the perfect tree, in the perfect place.

The rope swing was tied on with what looked to be a complex noose that wound its way about a quarter of the length down the rope. Whoever tied that rope knew exactly what they were doing. But no one knew who tied that knot. The swing had been there as long as anyone on the lake could remember. Even the really old people, many of whom were long retired and now lived at the lake year-round, couldn't remember when that rope swing was first put up. When I first started asking about it, they would all say something like, "It's always been there. I remember the first time I got up the nerve to climb up there. I was so scared ..." Then I would be stuck listening to a long story that for some reason included a lecture about what's wrong with people these days and how much they loved "penny" candies.

In case you didn't know, there was apparently a time when you could buy a single candy for one penny. And old people apparently think that is worth including in every story.

There were lots of theories about who built the Death Swing, but no one actually knew who tied that knot, or when or how. Whoever they were, they left an enduring legacy at Falcon Lake.

I wonder what they called the swing when they made it?

Maybe they were the ones that named it the Death Swing? Maybe one of the builders was the first victim, and the survivors chose the name? Whatever name they chose, whoever picked it, it was the perfect name.

First, a note on the body count. I don't know anyone who died because of the swing. But everyone at Falcon Lake knew someone, who knew someone, who knew someone, who did. If you ever mentioned the swing to another family at the lake, everyone had a story about one of the swing's victims. It was always someone not too closely connected to them personally but close enough that they knew all the gory details.

Sometimes it was a distant cousin who had invited a friend for the weekend. The cousin had a good swing and had entered the water safely but went too deep and never surfaced. Their body was never recovered and is probably still down there, stuck in the cold mud or wedged between some rocks at the bottom of Falcon Lake. When telling the story about this distant cousin, people sometimes said that if you dove deep enough, you could see the corpse, legs trapped in the darkness of the lake bottom, arms reaching up to the surface, trying to grab anyone who dove too far down.

Other times, it was a story of some teenagers who stole a boat in the middle of the night and headed out to ride the swing. It was really dark out on the lake, but the thieves didn't want to turn on the boat lights and risk getting caught. So, when the first teenager used the rope swing, they couldn't see where they were landing. Some say the teen hit the rocks at the base of the cliff; some say they landed in the stolen boat. Everyone agrees that the whole thing was covered up, since the dead teenager was the child of the local chief of police.

Occasionally, the story is of a young boy whose family used to have a cottage on the lake. Whenever I was told it, he was always "about your age" when he decided he was old enough to try the swing. But when he got to the top of the cliff, he chickened out and started crying. His father decided to motivate him to jump by telling him that if he didn't jump off the swing, he would have to walk back to the cottage. The walk would take hours, since his family's cottage was on the shore farthest from the swing. He'd have to walk around most of the lake. But the boy was too scared and opted to walk. The rest of the family boated back to the cottage, but as hours went by and night fell, the family became worried and went searching for the child. They searched all night before his body was found early the next morning, covered in rattlesnake bites. His family sold their cottage shortly after, and that's why you can't go knock on their door and ask if the story is true.

Which brings me to another reason the Death Swing is such a perfect name: all the ways it could kill you. You could be killed just getting there. Unlike the manicured grounds that surround the cottages, the area around the cliff is dense forest with lots of dead, fallen trees and thick undergrowth. It is the perfect habitat for the Massasauga rattlesnake. The Massasauga normally avoids humans; it is extremely rare for one of these snakes to initiate contact with a person. However, because of its excellent camouflage, you are very likely to step on it before you see it.

Plus, as a member of the pit viper family of snakes, it lives in huge nests that can have hundreds of snakes. And while the venom of one Massasauga is survivable, if you are attacked in the wild, you would likely be bitten by dozens or even hundreds simultaneously.

But let's say you make it to the swing unharmed. Then, there are plenty of ways that the swing can earn its name. When it's your turn to swing, as the rope returns from the last jumper in a slow, arching pendulum, you've got to lean out and grab the rope on its way back. Lean out too far and you will fall onto the rocks.

If you do manage to successfully grab the rope, you are still in danger. When you start your swing and step off the cliff's edge, gravity tries to pull you off the rope. Lose your grip and you will find an abrupt end on the rocks or in the shallow water, far below.

If you do manage to successfully hold on, as you come to the end of the pendulum's ride, you need to let go at the exact right time so that your body enters the water at the correct angle. With a fall from that height, you are travelling at a rate of about seventy kilometres an hour, so you need to get this right.

You want to land feet first, both arms up in the air, like a pencil dive. Any other approach could be deadly.

Legs tucked in for a cannonball? Your shins will take all the impact. You will break both legs and possibly your back too. You will not make it back to the boat.

Stick your arms out for balance? The force of the water will throw your arms up over your head as your body plunges under the surface of the water. You will dislocate both arms. You will not be able to swim back to the surface before you run out of air. Arms above your head is the proper technique.

Let go of the rope too late or too early, you are risking "death by belly flop." If you hit the water flat on your stomach or on your back, you are in for agony that most of us can easily imagine. Unlike imagining things like being bitten by a lion or stabbed by a samurai, we all have an idea of how much this would hurt. Most of us have belly-flopped before. Imagine that from the top of a cliff. Sure, the pain itself might not be enough to actually kill you. However, the pain might make you wish you were dead.

I knew all of these things.

I had heard about each of these dangers and more.

But still, I decided to do it.

I was eleven years old when I made up my mind.

Why would I choose to do something so dangerous? Something I have just explained was deadly?

Something so deadly that it took several pages to explain just how deadly it is?

'Cause I wanted to be a grown-up. I was tired of being a kid, the youngest in the family, the little brother, my parents' "little man." I wanted my family to stop thinking of me as a child. I thought the Death Swing would make me a grown-up, like my brothers, my dad, my uncles, and, it seemed to me, everyone else at the lake.

Not to mean that they pressured me; in fact, it was the opposite. Whenever I mentioned the swing, I was told things like "maybe next summer" or "one of these days." In fact, the idea that they did not pressure me is another example of how dangerous the swing truly was. When a big brother won't pressure a little brother into something dangerous, it means it is *extremely* dangerous.

On the first night of this trip to the cottage, I announced to my family that I was going to try the swing. I had expected there would be resistance. At least a little. But everyone seemed to think it was a good idea. My brothers were excited. My dad said that the forecast looked like a perfect day out on the water. Even my mom was on-board. I was sure she was going to try to talk me out of it, but she simply smiled and said, "If you think you're ready, sweetie."

I didn't sleep much that night. I lay in bed and made a mental list of the few things in the world that were more dangerous than the Death Swing. After a brief internal debate, I decided that the swing was the third most dangerous thing you could do. The Death Swing came behind only flying to the moon and jumping the Grand Canyon on a motorcycle. Eleven-year-old me reasoned that while astronauts and daredevils did things that were potentially much more dangerous, they had some important things going for them that I did not. They were adults, they were highly trained, and they wore safety equipment. I was not even a teenager, I had only ever been on playground swings, and my only equipment was a worn-out pair of Chip & Pepper swim trunks. I finally drifted off to the hope that the weather would change and my trip to the Death Swing would be delayed.

The next day, the weather was perfect, with a beautiful warm sun, not a cloud in the sky, and the lake was as smooth as glass. That meant a couple of things.

First, I could not use the weather as an excuse not to go on the swing.

Second, I could not count on my mother for a last-minute reprieve. She saw the weather as perfect for reading in her hammock. That meant she all but pushed us out the door so she could begin her "me time" as quickly as possible.

Third, the excellent weather meant that lots of other people at the lake had the same idea. By the time we got to the swing, there were already half a dozen boats anchored near the shore. It looked to me like most of the lake's residents were either in line to jump or watching from the water.

My dad manoeuvred the boat in to drop us off at the base of the cliff, well to the left of the swing. There sat a large, flat rock just above the water level of the lake, which made for the perfect place to get out of the water after a jump. From there, a trail of wide divots and flat ledges made a natural staircase up to the top of the cliff and the swing.

My brothers and I swam the short distance to that bottom step as my dad moved the boat to a safe distance and anchored. From this point on, it seemed to me that everything moved much faster than it should. We moved out of the water and up the stairs to the back of the line in an instant. About a dozen people were already in line for the swing. I saw this as a chance to try to relax.

I never even had a chance to stand still.

See, my older brothers climbed much quicker than I did and started chatting with the jumpers in front of them in line.

They explained that today was going to be my first time on the swing.

Those strangers began offering me their place in line. The residents of Falcon Lake were both generous and kind, much to my distress that morning.

I went from last in line to next in line in a heartbeat, which was incredible, considering how fast my heart was beating.

While I was stuttering about how "I wouldn't want to take anyone's spot" and how I was "happy to wait my turn," strangers ushered me to the front of the line. I bypassed the entire line and found myself standing at the edge of the cliff, watching the rope swing back toward me as the previous swinger splashed into the water far below.

My brothers noticed that I was frozen in fear at the top of the cliff and screamed, "Catch it!" as the rope was about to finish its return swing and loop back over the water. Shocked into motion, I leaned out over the abyss and reached for the rope. I grabbed a handful of threads from the frayed knot at the bottom and leaned back from the edge, pulling the Death Swing with me.

Yes, I had caught the rope, but barely. I had only the frayed bottom of the rope in my hand. Only then did I realize I wasn't big enough to do this.

Physically.

I was too short.

I couldn't reach the knot on the bottom end of the rope. Standing at the edge of the cliff on my tippy-toes, I could only reach as high as the frayed threads underneath the knot. I couldn't swing with the grip I had; I would fall straight to the rocks. There was no way I could swing like this.

Trust me, when dealing with something that has "death" in its name, you want to make sure you have a solid grip.

I had no choice. I couldn't do it. I had to climb back down. Dad would be disappointed. My brothers would pick on me. The story of the kid who "chickened out" would travel around the lake so fast that my mom would probably hear the story before we got back to the cottage.

But there was nothing else to do.

I would just have to wait until next summer. Maybe then I'd be tall enough.

I turned to give the rope to the next person in line.

I think it was someone's dad. I remember he had a blue swimsuit, a dark moustache, and a sympathetic smile when I looked over my shoulder at him. "That knot's a little high up there, eh, kid?" he said. As the closest one to me, he could see exactly what my problem was. "I was probably even shorter than you the first time I came up here. No worries, it happens." He gave me a wink as he walked up

I was saved.

A kind man at the lake had saved me from an early demise. He was going to take the rope away from me, and I would be able to climb down the stone stairs and then swim back to my dad on the boat. Yes, I'd have to walk past my brothers and dozens of others on my way down. Yes, it would be embarrassing, but I would survive. Because of one kind stranger at the lake, I would not be facing a desperate swing with a precarious grip. My young life would not come to a tragic end, like so many others. My body would not be broken or drowned like the dozens or maybe even hundreds before me that had not been given the same opportunity to walk away.

The kind man walked up behind me. "No worries, kid, I got ya," he said. Then he grabbed me by the waist and lifted me up off the ground. "Grab on, two hands," he said. Instinctively, I adjusted my grip above the knot. Then I realized what he was planning.

He was not going to save my life — he was going to help me die.

I turned my head around to look at him, but he was focused on my hands, making sure I grabbed the rope correctly. If he had looked at my face, he would have seen a person that was in no way ready to attempt a death-defying stunt. But all he saw at that moment were my hands, which apparently at that moment looked ready.

I wanted to say something about not being ready yet. But I didn't actually say the words out loud. I was so scared, so shocked, so terrified. I don't know if I was actually capable of making a sound. My throat was closed, and terror trapped my voice in my mouth. But in my head, I was screaming.

"Stop, wait, I'm not ready. Don't let go. Don't let go. Don't let go!"

Then he let go.

Since I was dropped while trying to turn around and look at him, I began to spin as soon as he let go. The rope began its arc, and I began to rotate. As I revolved, turning away from the cliff, I saw his face one last time before my gaze moved out over the lake. He was still smiling. A calm, pleasant smile, like someone who had just done a good deed. Like a Boy Scout who had helped a little old lady cross the road.

He was proud of himself.

He was obviously deranged.

Learning his motivation for murdering me would have to wait; I had more important things to think about. Gravity had immediately shown its authority and was trying to rip the rope from my hands and dash me against the rocks. I squeezed the rope as tight as my eleven-year-old hands could. I felt my knuckles crack and the rope compress in my grip. I had imagined this moment so many times. Thinking about how I needed to maintain the proper form. I needn't have worried. Gravity and a distinct lack of upper-body strength did most of the work. I took the ideal form of a "pencil dive" as gravity stretched out my arms above my head, I hung from the rope, and raced to the lowest part of the swing.

The spinning continued, and as I reached the bottom of the swing, I finished my revolution and saw the edge of the cliff. It looked incredibly far away. I was relieved to note that I was already past the rocks at the base of the cliff. I noted that I had avoided falling on the rock and could now look forward to a painless drowning. As I rotated away from the cliff, I saw him again, moustache, blue shorts, and yes, he was still smiling.

At this point in a swing, the world of physics has lots of complicated things going on. All I can tell you is that this part is where it is hardest to hold on. Momentum and gravity conspire at the bottom of the swing to tear your hands off the rope and send you to a watery grave. But this part of the swing was where I actually felt the best. My slow rotation gave me my first view of the landing zone, and I recognized instantly that I was headed for the right spot. I was well out of danger of the rocks and headed quickly for open water.

The building energy of the downward arc was spent, and now, as I passed the halfway point of the swing, that energy was released and I was hurled upward and away from the cliff. Racing toward the top of the arc, I remember thinking, *All I have to do is let go at the right moment … now!*

Then I kept swinging.

My brain screamed, *Now. Now. Now!*

But my fingers would not let go.

They were out of my control.

My hands thought that my brain had made a terrible decision.

They were taking over.

I continued upward.

I could clearly see that I was now higher than I had ever anticipated. I was at eye level with the branch that held the rope.

And still, I continued upward.

My momentum launched me above the Death Swing.

I kept flying upward.

I had swung so far and so fast that I was now looking down on the tree from above, then a pause.

I was weightless in the air. Above the top of the cliff, higher than the rope, beyond the top of the tree.

I was higher than anyone had ever been above Falcon Lake.

Then I let go.

The wind filled my ears as I began to fall. I saw the sunlight sparkling off the water. I saw the cottages in the distance like dollhouses. I saw our family's boat anchored offshore with a handful of other boats dotting this end of the lake. It was a moment of suspended peace.

Then I saw my father pointing at me and screaming.

I couldn't hear what he was screaming or locate what he was pointing at. But I assumed he was pointing and screaming at me because I was about to die. I couldn't see it, but it seemed to make sense that my father was trying to warn me about where I was about to land.

Maybe I was closer to the cliff than I had thought and was headed to an abrupt end on the rocks.

Maybe I was farther out than I thought and was about to make a terrible dent in someone's fishing boat.

Maybe a great white shark had made it into the lake and was sitting underneath me at that very moment with its jaws open.

In that flash, it seemed to me that any or all of those things were possible.

Then my feet hit the water.

I was entering the water correctly, toes pointed and arms above my head. But before my eyes dipped below the surface of the dark water of the lake, I was able to recognize one last thing. My father was yelling "*No!*" and pointing not at me, but something behind me.

Now, while the "pencil dive" is the correct body position for entering the water from a height such as this, it results in a precarious situation once in the water. Positioning your body perpendicular to the water and streamlining your entry means you dive very deeply. As a result, when I stopped sinking I was much farther down than I had ever expected. By the time I stopped moving toward the bottom of the lake, the pressure was crushing my head, and all the air in my lungs was being forced out of my mouth in a steady stream of bubbles. I was out of breath and very deep. I had no time to think about my father and his screaming and pointing.

I ascended as quickly as I could, kicking my legs and using my arms to pull me back to the surface. Just before I got my head out of the water, I remember thinking it had started raining. I could hear the rhythmic splashing as the scattered raindrops broke the surface of the water. It must have been a very sudden storm.

I came up and gasped for breath, coughing and spitting up water. Dad was still pointing, but he had stopped screaming. One hand was covering his mouth and the other pointed back toward the shore.

Back toward the Death Swing.

Or, I should say, back toward where the Death Swing used to be.

I turned around, treading water, still badly out of breath, and saw what had happened after I let go of the rope. As I was descending, so was most of the cliff. As I swung and had turned to face away from the shore, the cliff cracked and the top broke off. The large step at the top of the cliff separated and started to slide down the wall of rock. The cliff crumbled in a large circle that encompassed the entire top step and the one oak tree that grew out of the top.

Which had the Death Swing attached.

While I was underwater, swimming for my life, the side of the cliff was crumbling and falling into the lake. As I surfaced, the old oak tree, which had defied all odds and thrived in a place where it should never have succeeded, was sinking to the bottom of the lake behind me. By the time I turned to see what my dad was pointing at, the last limb of the tree was just dipping under the surface of the water, and behind it went the Death Swing.

The swing, which had been at Falcon Lake for longer than any living person could remember, was vanishing. The swing that had frightened and delighted generations of cottage-goers was sinking fast. The swing that had been tied by some ancient forgotten knot-master was disappearing into the abyss. The flat platform portion of the cliff was racing to the bottom, carrying with it the perfect rope on the perfect branch on the perfect tree. Like a giant fish that spits out your hook and swims away, the very end of the rope flicked its tail and dove under the waves, never to be seen again.

So that is the story of the first time I went on the Death Swing at Falcon Lake.

Also, that is the story of the last time I went on the Death Swing at Falcon Lake.

As well, that is the story of the last time, anyone, ever, went on the Death Swing at Falcon Lake.

ZOEY: A SUMMER CAMP LOVE STORY

OP HERE. SORRY IF THIS isn't the place for this kind of thing. But I could really use some advice. Anyway TIA for any advice you can offer.

Her name was Zoey, and she had no idea that I was the biggest loser in the whole school. It's true. That really was her name, and I really *was* the biggest loser in the whole school. That's not just my opinion. I had plenty of proof. In fact, I heard it at least once a day. The bullies. Coaches. That teacher no one liked. My older brother. Either at school or at home, someone was reminding me daily that I was the biggest loser in the whole school.

Just in case I ever forgot.

But not at summer camp. There, I was just another camper.

Unlike school, my older brother hadn't gone several years before me and cemented my reputation before I even got there. Unlike school, I didn't have my big brother preceding me at every step. I didn't arrive to find that star athlete, super-student, mister popular had gone before me. He hadn't paved a path that I could never follow and hadn't left me to be a giant disappointment to everyone I met.

I was never going to be him.

I was never going to make the basketball team, the football team, the soccer team, and be a track star. So why go to the tryouts?

I was never going to win every talent show, star in each school play, or solo in every school concert. So why bother auditioning?

I was never going to make the dean's list, be captain of the chess club, or lead the debate team. So what was the point in trying?

When I arrived at school, every teacher, coach, instructor, and recruiter sought me out so they could add the next "star" to their group. I could see the disappointment in their eyes the moment each of them realized I was not my brother; I was only me. That look was clearer than anything anyone ever said out loud. It said I was the biggest loser in the whole school.

But not at camp.

That was the very reason I wanted to go. To start fresh. In a group of strangers, I would find my own path.

But from the moment I boarded the bus to camp, I knew I was wrong. I realized everyone else had brought to camp the one thing I had forgotten: a friend.

Everyone else seemed to be attending with their best friend. Some people seemed to know everyone there, except me. No one knew me, and I knew no one.

So, when that first "free" period came up, everyone else had something to do and someone to do that something with.

Except me.

A "free" period was an unscheduled hour in the middle of the day when campers could do any camp activities that they wanted. There was an endless list. I could go swimming or horseback riding. There was an obstacle course and a rope swing. I could go canoeing or do a craft. I didn't want to do any of those things.

More accurately, I had no one to do any of those things with. I would have happily said yes to an invitation. But no one asked.

So I went for a walk.

Not that I wanted to be alone, but I thought it would look like I had somewhere to be. If people saw me headed somewhere, they might see me and think, *There is someone headed to join some friends*. And not realize I was the only friendless kid there.

The camp was huge, and because of that there were large maps placed around the grounds, hand-drawn with crude diagrams of the cabins, docks, paths, and dining hall.

The layout was pretty simple, with dozens of cabins on either side of the creek that ran through the middle of the camp, which separated the boys' side from the girls'. The "classrooms" (really just larger cabins but set up for crafts) ringed the eastern edge of the camp. To the west was Falcon Lake, where the canoes, kayaks, sailing, swimming, and water skiing happened.

At the start of that first "free" period, I saw other campers consulting a map near the dining hall, pointing to where they wanted to go on the map, and then heading off in that direction.

I watched as the crowd thinned. In happy groups, they would approach the map, quickly consult the diagram, and then sprint off saying things like, "Archery is this way, come on." Or, "The swim docks are over here, last one there has to swim naked," and laughed as they left. I lingered for a while, hoping for an invite. I imagined a group of three campers pointing to the tennis courts on the map and saying, "If we had one more person, we could play doubles." Then they would hand me the spare racket they just happened to be carrying and say, "Would you like to play tennis with us, and then we can all become best friends?"

It's interesting that my imagination had me both making friends and being good at tennis. I had never played tennis before.

My brother was a great tennis player.

No invitations came, and I was alone in front of that big map. I decided to head to where the kayak lessons happened. My thinking was that since a kayak was a solo craft, no one would question why I was there alone. Also, if there were other people who didn't have someone to hang out with, they might be headed there too, since it was a solo sport. I never made it to the docks.

I got lost. Almost instantly.

The long dirt road that I thought led to the kayaks went deep into the forest and away from the water. I wasn't really worried about making it to the kayaks; I reasoned there was no one waiting there for me.

I continued down paths that weaved around the forest and past wooden cabins, eventually realizing that everything from the map I had committed to memory was useless. None of the signs on the buildings matched what I had seen on the large map, so I kept walking. It wasn't like anyone was waiting for me.

Eventually, I noticed that the buildings were getting more spread out, and many of the ones I passed were boarded up and surrounded by overgrown grass. I was truly lost.

Then I heard noises to the right of the main dirt track I had been following. I wasn't sure what the sound was, maybe a campfire or someone barbecuing, but whatever it was made me think it was probably a person. I was no longer imagining a group of three friendly campers looking for a fourth. All I wanted was a camp counsellor who could point me to the docks.

But it was her.

She wasn't looking for the docks.

She was exactly where she wanted to be.

She wasn't hoping for an invite.

She was doing exactly what she wanted to do.

Curly black hair, tied back with a red scarf. Strong eyes, skin shiny with sweat. The first thing I thought of was Rosie the Riveter.

"Rosie" is an iconic poster from the Second World War that encouraged women to work in factories. In the poster, she is flexing her arm while looking directly at you. She is strong, powerful, and self-assured. Rosie wears blue, but this girl was mostly covered in beige. Thick beige overalls with full-length sleeves and pant legs. The silver snap-buttons on the front were done all the way up, and most of the beige was splattered with what I thought was reddish-brown paint. She had on brown work boots, also splattered with what I thought was paint, same for the huge black leather gloves.

Full-body brown, black, and dirty beige rarely makes for a flattering outfit. But for her it was perfect.

The gloves were massive and clumsy but exactly what you need when working with extreme heat. See, she was squatting down on the far side of a blackened metal garbage can that had a propane torch blasting flames into a hole at ground level. It's called a raku kiln. I didn't know that at the time; all I knew was that I couldn't breathe. Sorry. I know that is a silly phrase used in every romantic story, but I really was breathless. Shocked, surprised, stunned, and breathless, by the situation and her beauty.

Yes, she had great hair and beautiful skin and lips and neck and … well … everything. But it was what she was doing that took my breath away. She was so focused on her task that nothing else existed. Not the counsellors, not the camp, not even me, a few steps away, frozen in my tracks just around the corner of the building.

She was squatting, feet and knees pointed out, elbows anchored inside her thighs, fists balled up together and her chin resting on top. She was balanced, poised, like it was a yoga pose that she had perfected and could hold forever.

But more than that, there was a purpose. She needed to be positioned like this; it was the only way to be able to look through the flames and see the pottery inside. With eyes wide, all her attention, all her focus was on the flames blasting into the hole in the metal garbage can.

The side effect was that her brown eyes looked like they were filled with fire. Yes, they were beautiful too. But it was something more than that. It was the way she looked at the operation in front of her. She wasn't looking at her pottery project in the hope that it was going well. She wasn't staring into the flames to try to reassure herself she had done everything right. She wasn't crossing her fingers and wishing that her art would come out the way she wanted.

She wasn't timidly trying; she was fearlessly doing.

She was commanding the project to come out right.

She was in control. She was incredible.

Then the project got really interesting.

See, with a traditional electric kiln, potters use heat to cook the clay, normally at about twelve hundred degrees, then the art is allowed to slowly cool. A raku kiln uses direct flames but only reaches about five hundred degrees, and the creation is cooled very quickly.

This creates an effect that makes one-of-a-kind pottery. The process makes rich, vibrant colours appear in blotches as the clay is quickly heated then quickly cooled. Also, the rapid temperature changes mean that the piece gets covered with microscopic cracks that spread out like spiderwebs and make it instantly look ancient, fragile, weathered.

But this technique also means the piece could be destroyed. If the piece is cooled too quickly or has some invisible flaw, it could be destroyed at the very last step. The risk was extreme; hours or days of work could shatter in an instant. At the last moment, the artist leaves their final creation to fate. The sculptor may do their job perfectly, through every step of the process, but in the end the fate of the final piece is left up to chance.

It is an art unlike any other.

It is one-of-a-kind.

Like her.

It seemed to me that she stared into the fire for hours, but I had been lost in her eyes. Yeah, it's a gross cliché, but I could have spent days watching the firelight in her eyes. Sorry. Okay, no more. I'm done, I promise.

After a while, she had seen what she wanted in the flames, so she had to stop the process as quickly as possible. So, with those big clumsy gloves, she lifted off the silver trashcan and revealed the flame. Without the can containing it, the propane torch let out like a flamethrower in a war movie. Flames were spewing out across the ground, and the dirt on the space between us was instantly charred black by the flames.

My heart jumped into my throat.

I panicked. My mind screamed that I needed to run.

I needed to run and find an adult. There was no way she was allowed to be doing all this.

But then I saw how she was responding. She moved like she was building a sandcastle. Like, you're on the beach and you're having fun in the sand. You're concentrating and focused, yes, but there is no risk. There was no sign that she thought what she was doing was at all dangerous.

She was dancing from her table of tools to the fire pit.

She was calm, cool, and collected.

I was ready to run screaming for a grown-up.

I was Chicken Little. She was a hawk.

She took a long set of tongs, gently lifted the piece (it was a sculpture of a dancer), and gently lowered it into a low box filled with sawdust. Which, of course, immediately burst into flames.

Again, I was thinking about sprinting away to find an adult.

Not only 'cause what she was doing was so incredibly dangerous, you know, unsupervised flamethrower in the middle of the woods. But I was starting to think that I was going to get in trouble.

In my mind, she was going to get kicked out of camp for what she was doing, and I was going to get sent home for not telling someone what she was doing.

She grabbed a shovel and started dumping scoops of sawdust onto the flaming pile. Each time she shovelled more sawdust on, more flames spat out of the mound. But each time she shovelled, the flames peaked a little lower, until the mound covering the art was just a black, smoking pile of ash. Then she stabbed the shovel in the sawdust pile, turned off the propane, and looked at me.

Just for a second. Then back to work putting away her tools and gloves.

But in that moment, that one second when she looked at me, I fell in love. Those eyes that had been filled with fire and focus looked at me, and I fell. The ground disappeared from under my feet, I dropped down, and I was in over my head. There is a reason they call it falling in love. It is unintentional, accidental, unavoidable, and happens so fast, you don't see it until you've already hit the ground.

I wanted to ask what she was doing, I wanted to ask where she had learned it, but most of all (and I'm being honest here), I wanted to ask if she knew that I had to tell an adult about what she was doing. Yes, despite her beauty, my first and prevailing thought was that telling on her was the right thing to do.

Keeping one eye on me, not suspicious, more curious I would say, she moved to my side of the outdoor kiln and leaned against the wall of the building as she dug in the pockets of her overalls. She pulled out a lighter and a pack of cigarettes, put one in her mouth, lit it, and took a long, slow pull before exhaling the smoke through her nose. It filled the small gap between us and wafted away in the wind.

I was no longer scared of getting in trouble. I was now terrified.

While the camp rules did not specifically say that campers could not use flamethrowers, I feel it was implied. And while I reasoned that she obviously knew what she was doing with the improvised blast furnace, it was possible, very unlikely, but possible that she had permission to do what she was doing.

However, I knew there was no way that she was allowed to smoke. That was specifically mentioned in the camp rules. She could be kicked out just for having those in her pocket. Not to mention smoking there in the open without even trying to hide it. I told myself to make a mental note of what she was wearing so that I could point her out to someone in authority as soon as I made it back to camp. In case you are unsure, yes, my prevailing thought was still that I needed to avoid getting into trouble.

Then she spoke to me. "You're not going to narc on me, are you?"

I had no idea what she meant. In case you have no idea what she meant, she was asking if I was going to tell on her.

Which I totally was. As soon as possible.

But I didn't know what "narc" meant. I didn't know its meaning as a noun or as a verb. But I knew from the way that she asked that it was a negative thing. To "narc" was bad, and I instantly wanted her to think of me as "good." I wasn't going to "narc."

Whatever that was.

The silence was getting to be too much. I needed to answer, but I had no idea what I was saying. I tried to sound confident when I replied, "I would never … narc."

Silence.

"Pfff, do I look like someone who would … narc?"

A small smile.

"Me, narc? No way. I've never narced. Nor would I ever … ah … narc."

She held out the pack of cigarettes. "Do you smoke?"

"Yes, of course."

I had never smoked before. I didn't even know anyone my age that had ever smoked a cigarette. I didn't even know anyone whose parents smoked cigarettes.

But I said yes without thinking. Well, I was thinking about how much trouble we were going to get into, but I said yes anyway.

Luckily for me, it was a very mild cigarette, Vantage 13s Kingsize. I had seen enough bikers and gangsters in movies to know what to do. I took to holding the cigarette like she did, flicking the ashes like she did, and putting it to my lips like she did, but never actually inhaling.

I was terrified. But I was no longer too scared to speak. In fact, the opposite happened. I couldn't seem to stop talking. I asked about the pottery and the blowtorch, the trash can, the sawdust, the dancer. I just wanted to keep her talking, to keep her talking to me, to stay in her company. To continue to have permission to be near her.

Again, not just because of her beauty. More because of her, I don't know, is presence the right word?

On the first day of summer camp, she headed alone to the middle of the woods, fired up a blast furnace in a trash can, threw sawdust at a flaming piece of art, then had a cigarette.

We couldn't have been more different.

I was too anxious to say "hi" to a stranger. I went for walks hoping people would think I had somewhere to be. I failed at everything because I never had the guts to try anything.

We couldn't have been more different, but she was still talking to me.

I asked her name, she said, "I'm Zoey." Simple, exotic-sounding, like a fancy perfume. Only one word was needed, and it could refer to no one else. Like "Elvis" or "Pepsi."

She asked mine.

I replied, "Kenneth Rodney Michael St. Clair." Oh god, why did I say my full name?

She laughed.

I quickly added, "But everyone calls me Ken."

I started to think that there was something special about that place. Maybe the clearing we were in was magic, or wood sprites had put a spell on her so she would be fascinated by the next person she met. There was something at work. Something that had to have an otherworldly explanation. An explanation that was something other than she found me interesting. That was impossible.

We talked. She answered my questions. So I asked more.

She smoked. When she offered me a second one, I told her I was trying to quit.

I learned all about her and her art. She walked me through each step of the process. I really admired the idea that the outcome was left to chance (she said "the universe").

I didn't like art class because my pictures never turned out the way I imagined. She was creating works of art without being able to know what the final outcome would be. I was too scared to start, and she was leaving the ending up to "the universe." She explained raku is a Japanese word that means "happiness in the accident." I told her it was the most beautiful word I had ever heard, and she smiled.

It took a long time for the piece to cool, but I didn't mind. Again, there was no one waiting for me, and I would have stayed right there even if there was.

When she unburied the piece, I thought it was ruined. It looked to be a misshapen, twisted oval and it was covered in black ash. Then she started to brush away the caked-on layers of charred sawdust. Underneath was a jewel. The whole thing had the shine and colour of a gasoline rainbow in a puddle. Mixed in was dark emerald green and shiny sapphire blue. The thing glittered in the sun, and random patches of reflective black made the splotches of colour stand out even more. The shape was a full, flat base that swept up as it separated into two pieces then swirled back together as one at the top. It was a pair of dancers spinning in a twist of colour.

It was a still piece of pottery, but it moved. The surface was hard, but the colours were liquid. It was made of clay, but the long tendrils of cracks made it look like she had trapped wisps of smoke inside.

It was unlike anything I had ever seen.

I told her that, and she kissed me.

First the cigarette, then this. Apparently, it was a day for firsts.

The cliché is that I was walking on a cloud, but that's not how I remember feeling. I felt like John Travolta in *Saturday Night Fever*. If you've never seen it then, well, you haven't missed much, but Travolta's "strut" is excellent. See, in the movie, he's a nobody at home. He's a nobody at his job. But when he dances, he's someone special. So there's a scene in the movie when he leaves home and is walking to the disco, leaving a place where he's a nobody and going somewhere where he's a somebody. He is headed to a place where he is comfortable, where he is confident, where he is appreciated, and you can see all of that when he struts down the street to the disco.

So, yeah I strutted back to camp.

And that's pretty much how the summer went. We had our individual courses, and we ate meals with our cabins, but any other time, we were together. Most of the time she had a project underway that she'd work on in the "free" periods, and I'd follow along. She tried to teach me, but I would often get distracted and end up just sitting beside her, chatting while she worked. If she didn't have an art piece that needed attention, we'd just go for walks. We'd spend our time walking the same paths that I got lost on that first day, holding hands, occasionally stopping for a cigarette, often stopping for a kiss. It was perfect.

I remember other couples crying on the last day of camp. But not us. Lots of other young people had paired up, split up, got back together, and then moved on to someone new. But not us. We were together from that first day. When the buses arrived to take everyone off to their separate homes, we knew we would see each other soon. Never even really said goodbye, just a quick kiss, and then I got on my bus and she got on hers.

I never saw her again.

When I got back to the city and climbed off the bus, only my mom was there to pick me up. Odd, but I didn't think much about it at the time. As soon as we were alone in the car, she explained that she and my father were getting a divorce. My brother and I would be moving out of the country with my mom. She wanted to move back to the town she grew up in, wanted to move back into the house her parents had left her. When I got home, the house was already packed.

I knew I needed to write to Zoey and tell her what was happening. But by the time I figured out what I wanted to say, we were already on the plane. I sent the letter as soon as I could, and she called a few days later. We agreed it wouldn't work, being so far away from each other. We cried together on the phone a lot. I cried even more after she hung up.

So I guess that leads me to my question. Should I call her? Should I write to her? Message her online? What do I say?

Thanks for being my first kiss.

Thanks for being the first person to look at me and see me.

Thanks for not seeing what my brother said I was, not what my family said I was, not what I had been told I was over and over again.

But me.

She saw who I really was and liked me. Something I didn't even think was possible.

I didn't even like me until she did.

So should I reach out? Has it been too long? Would it be better to leave it as a beautiful memory? Contacting her would be easy. She's pretty famous on Etsy (her pottery is seriously amazing). I wasn't even looking for her; I was shopping for a gift and stumbled across her online. One second I'm trying to find something for my sister's birthday, then I see her name and I'm back at summer camp, seeing fire reflected in her eyes and walking like John Travolta.

I don't know if she'd want to hear from me. Her page has a "contact" button. I've hovered my mouse over that button lots of times.

Should I do it?

LSS — I fell in love at summer camp. It's been a long time since we spoke. Do you think I should contact them?

Edit: Fixed the spelling

Update: Yes, I quit smoking. It's a deadly habit, and I wish I had never tried it.

The mods can delete, if not allowed.

WINNIE, VICKY, AND PORTIA

THE SHOW OPENS WITH A shot of a wet green jungle. Slowly, the camera crawls across the jungle floor, as if the viewer is stalking something. Before we see the host, we hear his famous voice with its smooth British accent.

"There is a hunter in this jungle that is more venomous than any snake, faster than any shark, and smarter than any ape. It is aggressive, it is deadly, and it is brilliant. The greatest hunter in the natural world may be the Portia spider."

"I don't know about this one, Winnie. It looks a little scary," Vicky says to the black Labrador curled up beside her on the couch. With a quick turn of her head and short quiet bark, Winnie reminds Vicky that they don't talk when her show is on. "Okay, sorry. Jeez."

On the flat-screen, the narrator steps slowly into frame and speaks directly to the viewer. *"Resembling a collection of dried leaves, this small spider can be found in a vast territory stretching through Asia and most of Africa. On the surface, it would appear to be like most any other carnivorous spider.*

"However, it is more than just another carnivore; it is also a cannibal. The Portia spider is a very rare class of spider. Known as arachnophagic in the scientific world, which means that it hunts other spiders, but if you wanted a more literal explanation, 'arachno' is the Greek word for spider, while the suffix 'phagic' refers to 'something that devours.' That is not usually applied to animals. It is usually reserved for things that are unavoidable like rust or decay. But it is apt for the Portia spider, for when it hunts, it always kills.

"When we come back, we'll step into the incredible mind of the spider that specializes in hunting other spiders."

As soon as the show fades and the commercial starts, Winnie turns away from the TV to look at Vicky. Vicky doesn't need the signal. She knows the routine and is already heading to the kitchen. It's a routine that they have maintained since Winnie first came home from the shelter three years ago.

Every Friday night, the two of them curl up in one small corner of the large couch. A nature documentary on the TV — that's Winnie's pick. And during the first commercial, Vicky gets them snacks, plain saltines for the human and cut-up carrots for the canine.

Winnie is very picky about her viewing choices. She doesn't seem to like the underwater documentaries and will bark until the channel is changed. Then, after Winnie's show is over, Vicky will get them ice cream and put on a romantic comedy. That's her pick, but Winnie always gets to watch her show first. It's one of the many reasons why her nickname is the "four-legged dictator."

Every part of Vicky's life revolves around Winnie. She spends each lunch break eating in her car while she drives home to let Winnie out. She pays a small fortune to order Winnie's favourite brand of dog food. Winnie sulks for days if they run out. Vicky has missed countless overnight trips because the dog cries too much at the kennel. Even when she bought this house, she picked it because there was less vehicle traffic on Falcon Lake Road than on the other streets she was considering. She jokes with friends about how the dog owns the house; Vicky just pays the mortgage. But she doesn't really feel that way. She thinks of it as their life. Their home, their walks, and their Friday nights together.

The narrator's voice returns just as Vicky scrambles back with their snacks. She has to hurry; if she's late she will hear another short bark from Winnie. It means "you were late" in a language that only the two of them speak.

"The Portia spider is the elite hunter of the arachnid world. For its size, it has the largest fangs of any spider and produces a venom that is more toxic than any cobra. But fangs and venom aren't the Portia's most impressive features.

"This hunter's most important weapons are the largest eyes and the biggest brain in the spider world. Being smarter and having better vision, the Portia has a huge advantage when hunting other spiders. And unlike other spiders, the Portia does not spin webs. Instead, it uses its prey's web against it. As Dr. Wendy Thibeault explains ..."

The voice of the old English man is replaced by the image and voice of a young woman in a lab coat. *"When the Portia invades the web of another spider, it drops onto the web in a very specific way. It lands as a leaf would land. The web's owner feels the vibrations on the web, recognizes the landing of the leaf, and knows to ignore it."*

The English narrator returns to add more drama to the moment.

"Ignoring what it thinks is a harmless leaf will be a deadly mistake for the web-making spider, but the next move by the Portia begins to show its true brilliance. If the Portia spider needs to move closer to its prey, it waits until a breeze blows the web, then it moves quickly while its movements are masked by the vibrations caused by the wind. By the time the Portia is where its prey can finally see it, it is too late."

The narrator is silent while the screen shows the Portia leaping in slow motion. The smaller hunter lands on the back of the much larger spider. It flinches as the Portia's fangs sink into its flesh, then it freezes as the venom takes effect. As the hunter finishes the kill, the familiar English accent returns to try to keep the viewer tuned in during the upcoming commercial.

"However, if the tactic of landing like a leaf and moving with the wind isn't paying off, the Portia has a backup plan. When we return, a deadly spider that strategizes to use its prey's weaknesses against it."

Again, Winnie gives a short, quiet bark. It's slightly different from the bark she uses to say, "Don't talk during my show," or "I would like a snack," but only Vicky knows the difference. This one means, "I ate my snack too fast, you should share your snack with me." Vicky has heard this many times and is quick to respond by moving her bowl of saltines away from Winnie and saying, "Oh no. You always do that. You ate too fast. You're just going to have to wait till the show is over."

Winnie knows that when the show is over, when Vicky has picked her romantic movie for the night, they will share a bowl of ice cream. Not two bowls, one bowl and one spoon. Vicky knows it's unhygienic and the dairy isn't good for the dog, but neither cares. Vicky will get them a large bowl of French vanilla — Winnie prefers the good stuff — and they will share every spoonful as they watch the rom-com. One spoonful for Winnie, then one for Vicky. Winnie laps sloppily at the spoon but never spills a drop. When the spoon is clean, it's Vicky's turn.

Often, when she's watching her Labrador's long tongue wipe clean the spoon she is holding, she thinks about what other people would think of her Friday night routine. She imagines bringing home someone special, someone she really likes, and then they witness her spoon-sharing ceremony and she never sees that special someone ever again.

Ironic, really, since she picked Winnie up from the animal shelter, after numerous suggestions from her worried mother, in order meet more people. The idea was to meet someone at the dog park or while out for a walk. The idea was not to spend Friday nights at home talking to a dog, sharing a spoon. But, not that she would ever tell her mother this, Vicky wouldn't have it any other way.

The show comes back on, and Dr. Thibeault is in her lab, watching a spider in a glass box. We hear her calm voice again. *"The Portia has a unique hunting technique in the animal world. No other predator has been known to hunt the same way. The Portia spider can mimic its prey's favourite meal. If a Portia is hunting a redback spider, whose favourite prey is crickets, it will land on the redback's web undetected and then carefully pluck the strings on the web to imitate the movement of a struggling cricket.*

"The redback will then have to move quickly to ensure that its favourite meal doesn't escape from its web, but again, without the excellent vision that the Portia spider has, the redback won't know it has been fooled until it is too late. It really is a one-of-a-kind killer."

The narrator returns to hype up the next segment before going to commercial. *"Already blessed with superior weapons and intellect, but when we return, the Portia shows off its most ingenious hunting technique and establishes itself among the greatest hunters of the animal kingdom."*

"Whew, this one is intense, eh, Winnie?" Vicky says. The answer is another quick bark that Vicky takes to mean agreement, but it also easily could have meant, "Hurry up with more snacks." Wrapping both arms around the Labrador's thick, furry chest, Vicky pulls her companion onto her lap. Winnie knows this posture well and lies down on Vicky's lap. The dog is too big to sit like this; most of her hangs off the side of Vicky's legs. It's not really comfortable, and there's plenty of unused couch, but this is how they both like to sit.

"I can tell you," Vicky says, "I'm a little freaked out by this spider documentary. Maybe we could find one about cute baby monkeys instead." Winnie gives a satisfied sigh and lays her head down between her paws. Vicky relaxes.

Yes, the house is dark and empty, and yes, the show is scary. But she knows she has no reason to be afraid. As long as Winnie is around, nothing can hurt her.

The commercials are about to end when the doorbell rings. Winnie sits up on the couch and gives a loud, sharp bark toward the door before leaping off Vicky's lap and running down the hall. As Winnie's back paws hit Vicky's diaphragm and the big Lab bounds away, she groans as the air is forced out of her lungs, then slowly follows her dog to the front door.

By the time Vicky gets to the door, Winnie is sitting quietly facing the door and wagging her tail. Vicky knows that posture. It means the dog thinks there's something good on the other side of the door. Usually, this posture means a visitor Winnie knows; it is almost always Vicky's parents, and Winnie is always happy to see them.

But the DoorDash guy is her favourite. Even though it is never the same person twice, Winnie always knows when it is food.

However, while Winnie is thinking that there is food or family on the other side of the door, Vicky knows that it isn't. She has not ordered anything, and her parents are out of the country.

More than that, Vicky doesn't have the same feeling Winnie has. Vicky has a knot in her stomach. The voice in her head, the one that is there to keep her safe, is being very loud, telling her not to open the door. She reaches for the doorknob as the voice gets louder.

Vicky stops and leans to try to look through the frosted glass panel beside the door. It's there to let in sunlight, not for looking out of. She can only make out blurry images on the dark front porch. She thinks she sees movement, just to the left of what the frosted glass shows her. It could be someone shifting their weight as they stand to the left of the door. It could be the tree on the front lawn moving with the wind. She is about to open the door, then she remembers the app. She hustles back to the living room for her phone. Winnie barks at her to say, "Aren't you going to open the door? It could be food!"

Vicky answers, "One moment, I just wanna check. I just wanna check something." Grabbing the phone off the coffee table, she unlocks it and opens the app. And just as she thought, there is no one there. Through the fish-eye camera in the doorbell and the app on her phone, she can see the whole porch. No one. The motion sensor porch light is on, and she can see almost to the sidewalk in front of the house. Nothing. Maybe it's broken or the batteries are dying.

She notices the commercial is over and the show has begun again. She calls Winnie, who does not move. She tries again. "Come here, Winnie, we'll have ice cream."

Having heard the magic words, Winnie bounds from the door and runs back to her spot on the couch.

The narrator with the white hair and the easy smile is sitting in a lab filled with spiders in glass cases as he resumes. *"It is only in lab situations like these that scientists have been able to witness the most compelling hunting technique of the Portia spider. When it is unable to mimic its prey's favourite food, it goes to the next-best thing: finding that food and using it as a lure.*

"Here in the lab, the team has been able to witness the Portia spider collecting ants and dropping them onto the web of the Mexican redknee tarantula. Not fooled by the Portia's mimicry, the tarantula is unable to resist the struggling of its favourite food. The Portia's plan works perfectly; by the time the tarantula sees the Portia waiting behind the ant, it is too late. The tarantula has been fooled by the greatest hunter in the spider world. After the break, how this formidable spider seems to be able to use its knowledge of light and shadows to full effect."

Maybe because she knows the show will be over soon, or maybe because she is hoping that it will be over soon, Vicky gets up just as the commercial begins and heads to the kitchen. Yes, it may be too early for ice cream, but she knows that Winnie won't mind. Besides, she needs to take a break. The spider documentary, the broken doorbell, the big empty house. Everything tonight seems to have her a little on edge. Winnie is happy where she is, stretched out to occupy as much of the couch as possible, while Vicky opens the freezer and gets out the tub of French vanilla. Then, in an instant, Winnie is running and barking. It's a loud bark, and she quickly sprints to the back door of their bungalow. Vicky knows this bark well; it means only one thing: the neighbour's cat is in the backyard. Vicky has no idea why Winnie hates that cat so much, but she does. Other animals, like squirrels and birds, can enter the yard, and Winnie will only stare. But that cat is enemy number one, and Winnie ducks through her doggy door to chase it out of her territory.

"Shoot," Vicky says, slamming the freezer door closed. She heads to the back door, following Winnie. When she gets there, she understands a little better why Winnie is so upset. The cat is not just in the backyard; it is back there, howling. It must be wounded to be making this much noise. Vicky can hear the cat's yowl clearly by the time she reaches the back door. She knows that Winnie wouldn't hurt the cat. But she's worried about whatever has hurt the neighbour's cat. If it is still in the backyard, it might hurt Winnie too.

She swings the back door open and calls again for Winnie. "Winnie, come back here," but Winnie doesn't acknowledge her. Even though the cat has stopped howling, the dog just keeps barking into the darkness of the back of the yard. Vicky looks to the left of her large back porch to confirm what she already knows: the motion sensor lights aren't on. They are supposed to turn on whenever something moves in the yard. But they didn't. When the cat made its incursion into Winnie's territory, the light should have come on. Or at least when Winnie ran out, the light should have turned on. But the whole backyard is dark. The only light is coming from inside the house, thin, soft light from the kitchen window and bright white light from the open back door. While there is plenty of light coming out the doorway, the bulb is high on the ceiling and close to the back door. With this steep angle, it doesn't illuminate much of the backyard. The light cuts off in a sharp line at the bottom of the stairs leading from the porch, just before reaching the barking dog sitting on the grass. While Winnie is visible, beyond her nothing is. Vicky can't see what her dog is barking at or if there is even anything there.

Vicky walks to the edge of the porch, calling for her dog. "Come here, Winnie. Winnie, come here."

Vicky has never shouted at her dog, never. Not for chewed-up shoes or accidents in the house. Never. But she starts shouting now, 'cause she's afraid for both of them. "Winnie, get over here! Right now!" But Winnie doesn't respond. She doesn't move, she doesn't look back, she just continues barking. In fact, it seems to Vicky that her barking is getting louder and faster. If she had to guess, Vicky would say that Winnie's words have changed. When Winnie first ran outside, she was saying, "Get out of my yard," but now ... now Winnie is posturing, threatening, saying, "Get out of my yard, or I will hurt you." That would be Vicky's guess, but this is all new to her. She's never heard Winnie bark like this before.

Vicky is about to step off the porch and on the first of the two steps down to the grassy yard when she stops. The grass is wet with dew, and she's not wearing any shoes. She will have to go back in and get some. But she's terrified to leave Winnie out here. She can't explain why, but she's scared for Winnie to be alone in the darkness.

She begs, "Please, Winnie, come here, girl. Come back inside." But the barking continues.

Telling herself that she needs to be quick, Vicky scrambles back to the door, then grabs both sides of the door as she runs through and uses her arms to propel herself into the hallway, headed for the pile of shoes at the front door. She never really pays attention to the fact that the commercials have ended and the show has started again.

Turning right as she reaches the living room, she sees a close-up of the Portia spider on her TV. *"Maybe the most impressive technique this spider has is its ability to learn, adapt, and then pass on that information to other spiders. The Portia seems to be able to strategize and remember effectively. In one of Dr. Thibeault's experiments, a Portia was presented with an insect it had never encountered before, in this case a large beetle called the sand scarab. Its exoskeleton is almost impenetrable unless the spider can flip the beetle over and attack its soft underbelly. Through trial and error, the Portia is not only able to find the beetle's weakness, but it also appears to remember the vulnerability the next time it faces a sand scarab.*

"Scientists are at a loss to explain how the spider can do something only the largest primates are known to do. Dr. Thibeault has one theory...."

By the time the young arachnologist is back on the screen, Vicky is rushing past the TV, headed to the back-door wearing her sandals. Impractical for running, but they were the first thing she spotted in the pile of shoes just inside the front door. She turns her back to the TV, and that's when she realizes.

The barking has stopped.

Vicky races to the back door. She is sprinting so fast that she's risking losing the sandals that were so important just seconds ago. So fast, she can't even shout.

She wants to call out "Winnie," but her mind is only capable of doing one thing: telling her to move faster. Maybe if she can get there fast enough, she can stop whatever is happening. Maybe if she can get there fast enough she can stop whatever bad thing is happening. Maybe if she can get there fast enough she can stop whatever terrible thing is happening to her dog.

But she is not fast enough. Even though she is running as quick as she can. Even though she leaps from the porch, never even touching the two stairs that lead down to the lawn. She is not fast enough. Winnie has gone into the darkness.

When Vicky reaches the hard edge of the light from the doorway, she stops. She stares toward the back of the yard, but she is unable to see anything. She knows what is back there in the darkness. Nearby is a patio set and toward the back of her yard there is a cluster of trees. And somewhere in there is her dog, hurt and needing her help, but Vicky is terrified of stepping into the darkness.

A different voice in her head, the guilty one, reminds her that Winnie would not hesitate to help her; in fact, there is nothing in the world that would stop Winnie from helping Vicky. She tries to calm herself with a deep breath, but all she can manage is a shuddering inhale that leaves her feeling even less brave than before.

Vicky forces her legs to work and takes one large step across the boundary of the light from the door ... and that's when it hits her.

Blinding pain in the back of both feet. Like fire. Like she had stepped into a campfire without seeing it. Instinctively, she turns to look behind her, but she can't see anything.

She expected to see a pit of fire or lava, but there is only the line in the darkness a few feet behind her, a defined edge where the light from the backdoor ends and the darkness takes over. Then the line starts moving away from her. The light is jumping away from her as she moves farther into the darkness. Jagged, wobbly steps as she stumbles away from the safety of the light and the house and moves deeper into the darkness. The feeling of fire is gone now. Replaced by ... nothing.

From her shins to her feet she can feel ... nothing. She can't tell where her feet are or even if they are still attached to her legs.

Then she falls.

Staggering backward, her dead feet can't keep her up any longer, and she crashes onto her back. Her elbows slam into the wet grass when she lands, but they do little to slow her down, and her head slams hard into the ground. Almost as soon as her back is on the ground, she has that same feeling again: fire, this time in both hands at the same time. She has no choice but to pull her hands into her body and away from the flames that her mind says must be there. The pain and the fall have taken the air out of her. She can't get up. She can't scream. She can't call for Winnie to come and save her, even though she was there to save Winnie.

Then the sparks start to land all over her body. First, both thighs and her hips, followed by both shoulders and her lower back. Burning red embers bury into her skin, digging down to the bone with scorching heat and leaving nothing behind. No feeling. No sensation. No control. In seconds, she is immobilized on her back in the grass, in the darkness.

When the feeling of fire hits her chest, neck, and then her face, she wonders what will happen when the burning feeling is gone. If it burns down to her heart, what will happen? If the embers reach there, will she be able to feel it when it stops beating?

She knows what is about to happen. She knows that there is nothing she can do to stop it, but her last thought is not for her. The last thing she thinks is about Winnie, wondering who will take care of her.

Will they be good to her?

Will they feed her carrots?

Will they ever learn how she likes to eat her ice cream?

Inside, the show is still playing; the narrator ends the episode: *"With an intelligence to rival any animal and a greater collection of weapons than any other predator. We are very lucky. Out of the seventeen species of Portia spiders, we are fortunate that none of them hunt humans."*

FROGS AND FORTS

I WILL TELL YOU WHAT happened.

I will tell you everything.

I will. I promise.

I just hope you won't think I was a bad kid.

I certainly couldn't blame you if you did.

My old tree fort meant everything to me growing up. No, it wasn't much to look at, but it was my whole world as a kid.

I guess to other kids, things like who had the best marble collection or who had the best bike would have been important

But growing up, there were two kinds of social currency: frogs and forts.

Frogs might seem like an odd thing to boost someone's social status, but good frog catchers were highly regarded in the neighbourhood growing up. There is a skill to the task. It takes a fair amount of patience, so it was usually the older kids that succeeded. If a young kid was seen to be very good at the task of catching frogs, they were deemed more grown-up or mature than others. That's probably why "froggers" were held in such high esteem.

The best fort is a little easier to understand. Just like grown-ups who put effort into having the best car or clothes, having the best fort often meant having the most money. But since kids could scavenge things from almost anywhere for their construction, there was a sort of fairness in the forts. A kid whose parents had little money could still find a piece of plywood at a construction site, just as well as anyone else.

Having a good fort was also an example of how much "freedom" you had. Mine was, of course, not much more than box made of scrap wood sitting precariously in a tree in our backyard. But it was mine and gave me a solid footing near the top of the neighbourhood social ladder.

Which brings up another important point about having your own fort. Whoever built the fort made the rules. That kid (or kids) could decide who was allowed into the fort. Or more specifically, who was *not* allowed in the fort. Keeping someone out of your fort was a power play. By saying who could come in, you were drawing very clear lines about who was your friend and who was not. Yes, it is mean to exclude people, but it happened, and it happened a lot.

Quite often, it would result in a kind of "arms race" in the neighbourhood. If a child was excluded from the best fort around, they would often build one of their own. If that new fort was better, then neighbourhood kids would start to hang out at that new fort, and the owner of the new fort could exclude whoever they wanted. This would force the excluded party to improve their old fort to try and attract the neighbourhood kids to return. This pattern could be repeated all summer as forts got better and better.

"Frogging" was much more democratic and less likely to get a kid in trouble for stealing wood from a construction site or "borrowing" their parents' tools. Sure, there were plenty of mud-covered clothes and the occasional rubber boot that got sucked into the mud and had to be left behind. But "frogging" was much less likely to lead to trouble. It didn't require stealing tools or trespassing on private property. Most of the best places to hunt were easy to get to and on public property.

There was a good spot at the local golf course. Even though it was called Falcon Lake Golf & Country Club, there was no lake. It was just a large, shallow pond that ran along the edge of the property. We'd stick to the side of the pond that was on public property, and on hot days we'd catch lots of frogs.

The golf course was the perfect place for "frogging," with just the right depth of water, somewhere between knee and ankle-deep. Frogs need enough water to keep them hidden from airborne predators like birds and dry-land predators like foxes. However, the water can't be too deep. Very deep water can mean big fish. Largemouth bass and pike are particularly fond of frogs and usually live in deeper waters.

Another good reason for frogs to stick to the shallows is that deep water is often clear water. It is easier to hide in the mud and grass of the shallow water. But if a frog is out in the deep, clear waters of a lake, it is much harder for them to evade predators. If a frog wandered out to the deep part of a lake or pond, they would become more visible to the hawks or herons flying overhead. Plus, while frogs are obviously good swimmers, in the open water they lack the endurance to avoid a hungry fish.

Keep that in mind, not too much water and not too little, and you will find the best spots.

Once you choose the right location, you want to look for signs that show you where the frogs are in the water: air bubbles floating to the surface or tiny eyes looking out from the mud. If it has just rained, you might even see them along the shore as they leave the water and hunt for bugs inland. If it's sunny, you might find some of the bigger ones warming themselves on a rock or log.

Then you wade into the water, wait, and stand still. When you step into the water, all the nearby frogs will hide. But if you've picked your spot correctly, after a few seconds the frogs will begin to resurface. Remember, frogs don't have gills. They have lungs. They have to come up to the surface to breathe. And then you can catch them, if you remember one last thing.

Frogs can't jump backwards.

When you reach to grab a frog, it has only one way to move: forward. You can use that to your advantage. Most froggers will step behind a frog to make it jump away from them, and while it's leaping in the predicted direction, they'll scoop it up. Or if you have asked for the help of a friend (or insisted on the help of a younger sibling), you can have that person move behind the frog and drive them toward you. Some kids will use baskets or nets to catch the frogs, but the purists in the sport will just use their hands.

The size of your frog collection was also a sign of freedom. Most parents would not let their kids keep frogs in the yard, the typical excuse being warts. But if a kid in the neighbourhood was allowed to keep a small collection, it showed a maturity and trust that elevated them in the eyes of the other kids. No one ever kept their collections for very long. After a day or two, their parents would insist that the frogs be taken back to where they were caught and released. The frog catchers would usually say goodbye before opening the bucket or box they had been transported in. Often the "froggers" would say the frog's name as each was taken out of the container and placed on the water's edge.

"Goodbye, Jumpy."

"Goodbye, Slimy."

"Goodbye, Kermit."

"Goodbye, Lily."

"Goodbye, Mrs. Croakfire."

"Goodbye, Ribbit Downey Jr."

"Goodbye, Snoop Froggy Frog."

As I said, no one ever kept their collections for very long. But that is not entirely true. There was this one time.

See, I had the best tree fort around. At least for a little while.

At the beginning of the summer in question, I started to be very picky about who could and who could not come in. My best friends were always allowed in. Darren, Andy, and Jeff Marcella didn't even need to ask. But other kids were kept out. That weird kid with the glasses, I forget his name. I always sent away the other Marcella kids. Jeff had four little brothers, I think. It might have been five. Either way, Jeff was the only one I let in. I usually kept "the twins" out. They were two boys that lived in the neighbourhood, younger than me and therefore annoying. But sometimes their mom would send them over with candy to share. Those times, I'd let them in.

It was good to be king. But it didn't last long.

One day I went for a bike ride just to see what the other kids in the neighbourhood were up to, and as I rode past Jeff Marcella's house, I saw a huge collection of bicycles in the driveway. It looked to me like every kid in the neighbourhood was at Jeff's place. From the driveway, I could hear voices from the backyard and went back to investigate. That's when I saw the huge new fort.

Apparently, the Marcella family had built their fort in response to me and my fort. Specifically, for keeping Jeff's little brothers out of my fort. Apparently, the other Marcella boys had gone home and complained to their mom. When Jeff got home that night, he got in trouble for not including his little brothers. He explained that it was my fort and I was responsible for deciding who could and couldn't go in. To which his parents suggested that the Marcella boys could build their own fort in their own yard. The parents even offered to help. They bought some plywood, a rare and valuable commodity in the world of neighbourhood fort building, and even helped with the basic construction.

With a little bit of grown-up assistance, by the end of the next day, the Marcellas had the best fort around.

It wasn't a tree fort, but that didn't matter. Since it was on the ground, it was a lot bigger and it had strong walls and a solid roof. Inside, the entire floor was covered with patio stones left over from when the family added a deck the summer before.

On the ceiling, since theirs was not a flimsy tarp like mine, the Marcella family could hang lights. Sure, they were just old Christmas lights, but they gave the fort a special glow inside. Their fort not only had a big wooden door, but their parents had also installed a real working doorknob. They had a sort of top-hung window with a small shelf. It was a large piece of opaque plastic. With the hinges on the top, someone inside could open it from the bottom, prop it open with a stick, and then lean out onto the shelf, kind of like a lemonade stand or a stall at a farmer's market. But what these boys used it for was when their lunch was delivered. Jeff's parents would drop by the fort with deliveries of food for each of their boys. Each boy waited with the window closed, and when their parent arrived with lunch, they would give the "secret" knock (if the parent couldn't remember the "secret" knock, the boy would just shout it from inside), then the plastic flap would be opened and lunch would be delivered.

The lights, the door, and the catering. Their fort was easily the best.

After all the times I had excluded the younger Marcellas, I was lucky to be allowed in. In fact, Jeff's younger brothers argued loudly that I could not come in that day when I first arrived. But Jeff was one of my best friends and the oldest brother. He quickly explained that none of his friends were going to be turned away. As the oldest brother, his status in his family was secure. For that, I was very grateful.

We spent the next week or so of summer vacation playing in that fort. Before long, Jeff's parents were running a makeshift dining hall in their backyard. They had quickly abandoned the custom-made sandwiches they had started serving and switched to spaghetti. Much cheaper and easy to make in large batches.

They must have been feeding half the kids in the neighbourhood. Before the end, they had even set up a temporary dishwashing station outside by the garden hose. But "Marcella Castle" did end, rather abruptly, and I was the last one to know.

I started to notice that Andy, my other best friend, wasn't around as much, so I rode to his house one morning. His dad explained that they had some family who were in town for the summer. They had bought a house on the nearby lake, and Andy was spending time there with his cousin.

Shortly after that, I noticed that fewer kids were hanging out in the Marcellas' fort. Then I arrived one day, just before lunch, of course, at Jeff's backyard, only to find it was empty.

Then I discovered the whole neighbourhood was empty.

I rode around for the rest of the day, looking for any other kids. I rode to all my friends' houses — nothing. The park, the basketball court, the local pool. Nothing.

I even rode across town to check the comic book store and even the skate park, places where we rarely hung out.

Then I started going to all the places we were strictly forbidden to go (and therefore would only go occasionally): the train tracks behind the woods, the city dump, a quarry near the golf course, and the burned-down factory on the edge of town. It was forbidden, dangerous, and haunted, which made it an extremely tempting place to visit.

I even went and looked in the windows of the school. Honestly, I had started to think that the summer was over and no one had told me. But it was still locked up and shut down for the summer. All the lights were off, the chairs were upside down on the desks, and teachers were away doing whatever it is that teachers do during the summer (no one knows).

The next day, I headed back to the Marcellas' and knocked on the door. Mrs. Marcella answered and explained that all the boys were playing with Andy's cousins. They had bought a big place on the lake. She was surprised I had not been invited.

I was surprised too.

Every one of my friends had gone to play at someone else's house. And they hadn't invited me.

I was crushed. I felt like the last kid left on the whole planet. Like the Earth was doomed and the spaceship that was headed off to find a new planet just left without me.

I rode my bike around, not really thinking about where I was going. But my ten-speed knew where I wanted to be.

I was at the lake in less than an hour.

Finding Andy's cousin's house on the lake was very hard. They all looked the same: big. I rode past these big houses, not really knowing what I was hoping to see. I rode past things our neighbourhood didn't have, like gated circular driveways, three-car garages, guest houses, statues in the gardens, and some even had huge fountains built on the front yards. Because these houses were on the lake, every one had a dock and a boat. I didn't know it at the time, but everything I was seeing was the grown-up currency along the lake. Their houses and boats were our frogs and forts.

The one thing I didn't see was the one thing I was looking for: kids.

In our neighbourhood, it was easy to spot the houses where kids lived, like bikes lying on the front lawn, huge chalk drawings on the driveway, Tonka trucks in the flower garden and, of course, a fort built in the yard. But in this part of town, there seemed to be no sign of any kids anywhere. I was about to give up and head home when I decided to check out one last house.

That's when I saw it.

The greatest tree fort I had ever seen.

The greatest tree fort *anyone* had ever seen.

It looked like a pirate ship had been impaled on a giant oak. It was bigger than any fort (in or out of a tree) I had ever seen. The hull (the bottom of a ship) was made of dark red wood, and the planks curved away from the bow in a brilliant display of craftsmanship.

The bow faced the road where I sat on my bike. It had a long flagpole pointing out the front and was currently flying a long, thin flag. I would later learn it was called a *pennant* or a *pennon*. On both sides of the ship/fort, there were round porthole windows ringed with shiny brass, plus a balcony with a short white railing.

The left side (called the port side) had a long rope ladder with smooth wooden rungs, and beside that was a pair of swings that hung a massive distance from the bottom of the ship to the ground. The very long ropes meant that a kid on that swing could swing farther and swing higher than anyone at any school, park, or playground. It looked very dangerous, and I could hardly wait to try it.

The other side (starboard) had a tall cargo net for climbing. Like the swings, it ran a huge distance from the ship's railing to the ground. Like the swings, it looked very dangerous and very tempting. The starboard side also had the top opening of a yellow curving tube slide that coiled around the base of the tree three times before letting out at the ground.

The stern featured the most incredible things. Things I had never even imagined on a fort. All the afternoons and sleepovers when my friends and I daydreamed out loud about the forts we would someday build. None of our imaginations came up with these things.

First, a kind of dumb waiter. Basically, a tiny elevator, not for people but for any small stuff you wanted to move quickly from the ground to the fort. You could load the items into the box on the ground, and then you'd ring a hand bell to signal the people in the fort. They would use a crank to haul up the box, which was connected by a rope. The crank was part of a tall crane that could swing left and right on a pivot. That meant the cargo could be unloaded to a number of places on the lower railing or even up to the very top of the ship.

The other feature was a taut wire that ran from the ship down into the water. It was a zip line that allowed kids to jump off the back of the tree fort, zip across most of the yard, and splash into the lake. The handle, which looked like something a waterskier would use, could be retrieved by the person waiting for their turn up on the ship. Running parallel to the zip line was a thin cord. By pulling on it (like a clothesline), the handle could easily be retrieved and used again. And that's what my so-called friends were doing. I watched from the road as Andy, then Darren, then Jeff Marcella each took a turn zipping from the back of the ship into the water and then raced back to the rope ladder to climb back up to the fort and do it again.

The other Marcella boys were there too; they were scrambling up and down the cargo net. Darren had brought his sister, who was on one of the two swings. She, with Andy's little brother beside her, swung in huge arcs that finished unbelievably high off the ground. They were almost flying.

Out of the curving yellow slide poured an endless stream of kids from my neighbourhood. The Myres kids, the three Rogers boys, and even the annoying twins I mentioned, Jon and Josh, were there.

I sat on my bike. Astounded. Awestruck. Jealous.

Then it got worse.

A woman walked out of the house. The house was of course huge and gorgeous, but I was only interested in the fort that had taken away all my friends. The woman carried a tray filled with treats and headed to the dumb waiter. Into the little box on the ground, I saw her put in cookies and drinks. Not just homemade oatmeal raisin cookies and watered-down Kool-Aid like moms in our neighbourhood would serve. These were store-bought cookies, double-stuffed Oreos, and cans of Coke. She added the treats to the dumb waiter and rang the hand bell to signal that the delivery was ready.

That's when I saw him.

Standing at the very top of the ship on the bridge, behind a large steering wheel (the helm) was a boy about my age. He looked about as different from me as he possibly could. I was wearing a hand-me-down T-shirt (sweaty from the long day's ride). He had on a buttoned-up shirt that had obviously been ironed. I had jeans that had been cut at the knees to make shorts (jorts). He wore light khaki shorts that also looked like they had been ironed. I had sweaty hair that was last cut the day before school pictures were taken and would not be cut again until I headed back to school in a few weeks. He was wearing a yacht captain's hat. It was white, with gold trim and a shiny black brim. As soon as I saw it, I knew what it meant. He was in charge of the fort.

I approached cautiously, leaving my bike on the edge of the road and leaning up against the fence. I had decided against riding into the backyard; it seemed too bold. In this neighbourhood, I was (at best) unsure of my social standing, although considering I had been abandoned by my friends, the same could be said about my standing in my own neighbourhood. I walked around the fence with a big smile on my face. I walked slowly toward the "captain" with one hand raised in greeting. I thought I would mention my friends who were already inside the fort as quickly as possible.

But I never got the chance.

As soon as he saw me, the "captain" reached over to a bell that was attached to the railing beside the helm. He rapidly pulled on the rope and started clanging the bell while yelling, "Attack, attack, we are under attack. Man your battle stations!"

As he bellowed, the fort came alive with activity. Everyone stopped playing and sprinted to their assigned task. The dumb waiter was hoisted up onto the deck. The handle from the zip line was retracted and tied in place. People inside the fort pulled in the ropes for the swings until the wooden seats were flat against the underside of the hull (fitting perfectly into a recessed gap made just for this occasion). A large wooden board was lowered into place at the top of the twisting yellow slide, sealing it off. Every kid who wasn't already up in the tree fort was scrambling up the rope ladder. They streamed up it like ants climbing up the stem of a tall plant.

My ex-friend Darren took up a place at the top of the rope ladder. When each climber reached the top, he handed them a foam pirate sword out of a nearby toy chest. He then directed each of them to hustle, sword in hand, to what seemed to be an assigned position along the white railing that swept down the two sides of the ship. The kids that were directed to the starboard side of the ship made quick work of the cargo net. Moving in unison, reaching hand over hand, they drew up the rope net and quickly stored it on the other side of the low railing.

My former friend Andy was stationed at the bottom of the rope ladder, shouting at the climbers to "be quick" and "head to their stations." I started to head in his direction, hoping he could get me in the fort or at least explain what was going on. He never even looked at me. When he was the last one on the ground, he unlatched the rope ladder from a hook built into the ground and began scrambling up. The connection at the bottom kept the rope ladder fairly rigid for the other kids, but unhooked it swung and swayed while Andy climbed. However, it didn't seem to slow him down. He climbed steadily as the rope ladder turned and twisted, as he neared the top and was pulled up the final step into the fort. Clearly, he had practiced this climb. Unseen hands reeled in the rope ladder as soon as he was safely on board. Sealing everyone inside, and me (just me) on the ground.

I tried to call up, shouting my name (I was thinking that the kids from the neighbourhood simply didn't recognize me), but it was no use. The fort was teeming with activity, and the "captain" was far from finished ringing his bell and yelling orders.

To me it was nonsense, but everyone on the ship/fort seemed to know what he meant. I backed away toward my bike while he shouted, "Quarter gunners, load canister-shot and run out the guns!" which seemed to be the order to bring out three laundry baskets filled with water balloons from somewhere in the hull. While that was happening, he shouted, "Colour Guard, post the colours," then Jeff Marcella (who I had once considered one of my best friends) led a small group of younger kids to remove the white flag at the bow. They replaced it with a black pirate flag. Then the "captain" tucked a foam sword into the belt of his khaki shorts and shouted, "All hands, prepare to repel boarders."

They had declared war on me.

I backed away.

While I was in no danger and they were only armed with foam swords and water balloons, I had never seen kids behave like this. They had moved with military precision, often working in perfect unison to complete their tasks, and each of them was now standing at attention at their assigned station, ready for their next command.

They weren't neighbourhood kids.

They were disciplined and efficient. It was scary.

I shouted up and tried to introduce myself but quickly realized it was pointless. I didn't doubt they could hear me, but I could tell they would not do anything that the "captain" did not tell them to do. I doubted they would even look at me, unless they were commanded.

The "captain" was pacing back and forth on the bridge, eyeing me and occasionally speaking to one of the young kids lining the railing of the ship. When he did that, the kid would immediately stand a little straighter and salute without turning around.

After a little while, the "captain" apparently called a meeting. After barking for the "quartermaster," "boatswain," and "master gunner," I saw the three people that until recently had been my friends gather at the top of the closed-off ladder.

I assumed they were talking about me.

I was right.

After a brief conversation — not really a conversation since the "captain" seemed to do all the talking — the command was given. Darren and Jeff removed the board that sealed off the yellow slide. Then Andy was sent down.

He looked at his feet as he exited the slide and continued to look down as he headed across the lawn to where I was waiting. I knew I was not going to be allowed onto the ship. There it was, the greatest tree fort in the world, and I was never going to see the inside. That's what kept going through my mind as Andy explained the situation.

Obviously, this was the house that Andy's relatives had bought, and the "captain" was his cousin. Andy said he had tried to get his cousin to allow me in, but he had refused.

I had to respect that. The boss of the fort decided who could enter. It was the rule at my fort.

Also, just like my fort, there was a way to earn admission. But it was so much more than bringing some good candy.

To get into the fort, each kid had to prove themselves a loyal sailor.

Each new "recruit" would be given a task to perform in case of an "attack." They would then practice that task until the "captain" was satisfied, and they could join the crew. Several times a day there would be a "drill," and depending on how well each person did, they could be promoted or demoted.

Do well and you could be assigned a new title and a new job. Andy, my no-longer-friend, explained that earlier in the day, one of the younger Marcellas had made the rank of "Colour Guard" and joined the team that changed the flags on the ship.

With each rank, kids were allowed to play in different areas of the yard. Members of the colour guard were allowed on the climbing wall, for example. The members of the "senior crew" (Andy, Darren, and Jeff Marcella) were the only ones allowed to use the zip line. Kids who were demoted would find they had the less desirable job. If they failed those tasks, they were "marooned," which was a fancy way of saying "told to go home."

I had to admire what his cousin had created. He not only had the greatest tree fort in the world, but he had also used that incredible amount of social clout to control everything around him. Playing in his yard meant he decided who was allowed to play, when they were allowed to play, and where they were allowed to play. He wasn't just the "captain" — he was the king.

However, drills were designed to prepare the crew to repel an attack. Without an enemy, the game could not really be played. Unfortunately for me, Andy's cousin had decided that it was time to play the game, and I was to be the enemy.

Andy mumbled "sorry" and started to walk back to the fort as the rope ladder was being lowered. I thought I could plead my case a little more and began to run to catch up with him. As soon as I did that, the "captain" gave an order and the rope ladder was immediately retracted. It was simple: Andy could go up but I could not. I walked back to my bike and watched as the ladder was lowered and my no-longer-friend climbed up.

My heart was broken. I rode home.

The next morning, the neighbourhood was empty, and I once again found everyone at the tree fort. I never even stopped my bike. As soon as I was spotted, the alarm went off and the fort was locked up tight. This time I heard cheering as I rode away. They were celebrating their victory.

I spent the day alone. Riding around the neighbourhood. Thinking.

Thinking that I couldn't compete with a fort like that.

I was never going to have one like that. But there was one way I could compete.

The next afternoon, I rode to Andy's cousin's house. It was difficult and a slow ride with two buckets hooked on my handlebars, one on each side to try to balance the weight.

I spilled a lot of the water, but I made it. As expected, the fort was locked up before I even got close, but their expressions had changed. I could see, especially on the faces of the young kids who were at their posts along the railing, that they wanted to know what I had in the buckets. I got the feeling that the "captain" thought I was armed with water balloons, but that would have been foolish. With just two buckets of ammo and just one person throwing, I was outmanned and outgunned. He knew that, but he had this master gunner (Darren, the person I had once called a friend) distribute the water balloons anyway.

He was ready for a fight.

But maybe not ready for frogs.

I had spent that morning catching frogs. I had managed to gather two buckets of the tiny amphibians with a couple of whoppers added in as well.

I rode to the beginning of the huge driveway in front of the huge house, carefully dismounted, and carried the two heavy buckets onto the lawn. When I was close enough that I felt everyone could see me, I set them down and started to show off what I had collected.

I took the biggest ones out first. I'd hold them up over my head for the neighbourhood kids to see (there seemed to be even more than last time) and then place the frog gently on the ground. Then I'd grab another, lift it up high so they could see it clearly, and add it to the ones on the ground. By about the third or fourth frog, I could hear some gasps and murmurs from the ship.

My plan was working.

One after another, I pulled the whoppers out of the buckets and set them free on the lawn. Finally, when there were only the small frogs left, I dramatically kicked over the two buckets, and the crowd cheered when the water and frogs splashed out on the grass. Granted, the cheer was only from a few kids, and it was very brief, but it made me feel that I had made my point.

I had something I could contribute.

Something the "captain" didn't have.

Something of value.

I was sure I was going to be allowed up in the fort.

Then the "captain" yelled, "*Fire!*"

Water balloons rained down around me, exploding on the lawn, scattering my frog collection in all directions and chasing me back to my bike. I rode away as fast as I could, not stopping until I reached the top of the hill that overlooked the lake and separated the rich neighbourhood from mine. When I stopped to catch my breath, I looked back to the fort emptying behind me. Kids were popping out of the bottom of the giant yellow slide, one after another. Each one was sent down at a regulated pace to leave just enough space for the person at the bottom to exit the slide. When they reached the ground, the "sailors" began to collect the frogs I had worked so hard to gather.

I had nothing left.

No friends.

No frogs.

I had even lost the two buckets.

I had no way of getting inside the greatest tree fort ever made.

I stayed away for several days but eventually found my way back. I found a place on the hill where I could see the fort and watch its happenings without being spotted.

What I saw broke my heart.

They were frogging. All of them.

They worked in groups, while a few (including the "captain") remained back at the fort. But most of my "once-upon-a-time friends" headed off on their bicycles to catch frogs. I watched them ride off, each with an identical bucket with a handle and a tight lid. No doubt, Andy's uncle and aunt had bought them just for this purpose. I watched as they rode back to the tree fort and approached an aluminum rowboat parked under the tree.

It had not been there before.

There was a small group of kids stationed at the boat. When the froggers arrived, they worked together with precision. The boat was covered by three sheets of plywood. While a team of kids lifted up the middle sheet, another team emptied the buckets of frogs into the boat.

A third team, made up of the smallest kids, was tasked with collecting any frogs that jumped out while the new ones were being added. When the last of the escaped frogs were put back in the boat and the plywood lid was safely back in place, the froggers collected their empty buckets and headed off again.

I watched this happen again and again that morning, and I grew angrier each time the froggers came back. Not at the "captain." I wasn't mad at Andy's cousin; I respected him. He had breezed into town without really knowing anyone and made himself the most popular kid around. He was probably as unhappy about moving to our town as I was about losing my friends. But he saw an opportunity and seized it. Sure, he had the advantage of having his parents build him the world's greatest tree fort, but he had made the most of that.

When he realized the neighbourhood value of what he had, he had created an imaginary pirate crew, of which he was the commander, and everyone played along exactly as he dreamed.

When that was threatened, when I threatened what he had made, he used that "tree fort wealth" to grab the next most valuable thing: frogs.

I admired him. I envied him. I hated him.

But I was not angry with him. I was angry with the froggers.

Since there were no frogs to be caught at the lake, they had to head to my part of town. They were frogging in my neighbourhood. They waded into my ponds. They were showing other people my secret spots. They were catching my frogs.

I knew what I needed to do.

I went home and asked if I could sleep over in a tent in Andy's backyard. Yes, it was a lie.

I took some homemade oatmeal and raisin cookies, then I rode to my secluded place on the hill and watched. The sun was just setting. I had arrived just in time. The last of the "crew" were disembarking and headed to their homes. The "captain" went inside, and I watched until each of the lights in the house went out. Then I set the alarm on my Seiko watch for two hours and nodded off.

When the alarm shook me awake, I went to work.

The plan was simple: set the frogs free.

Since there was nothing I could do about the fort, it would have to be the frogs. I figured he had come by the fort honestly, but he had stolen the frogs. The fort was a work of art, and I would never dream of damaging it. The frogs were wild animals and meant to be free. The fort had been purchased by his parents, and the frogs had been kidnapped from my neighbourhood. Like my friends, the frogs did not belong here. They should be back where they belonged.

I meant to simply overturn the boat and let the frogs go free, then head home. I had planned to sleep in my tree fort, and then no one would know I hadn't been to Andy's.

But when I got to the boat, it was too heavy for me to tip over.

Plan "B" was to pull off the plywood sheets to let them jump out. When I moved the wood, none of the frogs moved. It was late at night and already very cool outside, so none of them were moving. Without warm mud to hide in, their amphibian bodies shut down in the cold water in the bottom of the boat. There were too many to take out by hand; it would take hours. I would have to do something else. When I saw the thick white rope at the front (bow) of the rowboat, I got an idea. If I could get the aluminum boat to the water, I could flip it over easily and free the frogs. However, moving the boat was extremely hard.

The aluminum boat itself was very light, but with a deep layer of water and frogs on the bottom, it was incredibly heavy. At first, I tried to push it. With my back against the flat part of the back of the boat (that's called the transom), I could dig in my heels a bit, but my footing slipped out from under me as soon as the boat started to budge. The cool summer night meant the lawn was already slick with dew. The same thing happened when I pulled on the rope. I could get a little bit of movement, but the wet grass made any significant progress impossible. I would need a new plan.

I scanned the yard, hoping for a miracle. I don't know what I wanted to see, but it didn't matter. There was nothing useful there. I was alone in the dark. Trespassing in a stranger's yard. With a boat full of frogs. It was time to reconsider my actions. I put the plywood covers back on the aluminum boat and decided to leave.

As I walked back to my bike, which was parked at the fence, wheels pointed at the road in case I had to make a quick getaway (I thought I was being clever), I spotted a spade with a long wooden handle. Apparently, Andy's aunt or uncle had been gardening in the afternoon and left the spade leaning against the corner of the house. As I passed it, I thought of school for the first time since the summer break had started.

One of the last things I remember learning was about the six simple machines. I couldn't remember them all. But I knew one was the lever.

I raced back to the boat and tied the rope to the spade. I secured the knot low on the shaft and drove the pointed end as deep into the lawn as I could. I then stood on the back edge of the blade and used my weight to bury it deeper. When it was in as far as I could get it, I held on to the top of the handle and leaned back as far as I could. As I fell to the grass in the direction of the lake, the spade came with me, pulling the rope, sliding the boat.

It only moved a little, but, thanks to leverage and gravity, it was almost effortless. Also, instead of stopping me, the wet grass was now helping as the boat slid toward the edge of the lake. I did this dozens of times as the simple machine helped me with my task. When the lawn began to slope toward the water, I was able to take advantage of another "simple machine," the ramp.

As the boat began to lean downhill, my work got much easier. I moved the knot holding the rope farther up the wooden shaft, away from the fulcrum, and was able to pull the heavy boat much farther with each tug. The heavy water in the bottom of the boat began to pool at the front of the boat and helped me slide it closer to the shore. Before long, the boat reached the wet sand on the edge of the lake and the keel, the centre part of the hull of a boat, made a satisfying splash. I pulled the plywood planks off quietly and set them on the shore. Then I pushed the boat out into the water.

I waded out with the boat, and the water got very deep very quickly. I was well past my waist when I grabbed the side of the boat with both hands and began to rock it back and forth. I couldn't get enough leverage to flip it and dump the frogs; I would have to spill them out.

I hopped up to put my weight on the edge of the boat. The far side of the boat rose up in response, and the water and frogs began to flow toward me. I had to lean almost all my weight on the edge of the aluminum boat to keep it below the waterline, but it was working. Hundreds, maybe thousands of frogs were pouring out in a steady stream, along with a small trickle of mud, grass, and leaves that the kids had added to the enclosure.

The first ones out were some of the biggest, giant whoppers with fat bodies and huge back legs. I could see them waken as they got used to the warmer water of the lake. After initially floating on the surface for a few seconds, the monster frogs would start to kick as they acclimatized. The clear water and the light of the moon meant I could see as each one "woke up" and started to swim.

I remember feeling good as I watched the first few frogs splash into the water. As the flow of frogs went from a trickle to a flood, I felt good about myself, and I felt good about what I was doing. They were trapped, and I was giving them freedom. They were my frogs, they were from my neighbourhood, and I was putting them back where they belonged.

Then it started.

First, just one fish.

Then a second.

A pair of largemouth bass had noticed the first whoppers hit the water and had come to investigate.

As they moved in, the last of the frogs poured out of the boat and into the crystal-clear and very deep waters of the lake.

I watched as the last little frog dropped out of the boat and started to swim, but it all started before I could react.

In seconds, the water in front of me was turned into a frothing storm as every fish in the lake converged on the buffet of defenseless frogs. Half asleep as they hit the lake water, without mud or grass to hide, pursued by agile predators in their natural environment of the clear deep lake water, the frogs, *my* frogs, had no chance.

I was driven back by the thrashing tails and fish bodies that slammed against me as hundreds, maybe thousands of fish dove into the spot where I had emptied the boat. I saw bass grabbing some of the whoppers, chomp down, and then plunge back into the swarm to continue the feeding frenzy. I saw small frogs being swallowed two at a time as a pointy-toothed pike picked them off. I saw frogs fling themselves into the air in a desperate attempt to avoid their violent fate, only to be pulled back into the water in the jaws of hungry carp.

It was a massacre, and it was all my fault.

I fell backward onto the shore as the feasting fish turned the water in front of me into a boiling nightmare of fish and frogs and water and blood.

Then things got worse.

The boat was taking on water. Having dipped the side of the boat to let the frogs out, I had let the water in. I saw the bow of the boat dip under the surface of the water, and it rapidly filled with lake water. Before I could even think about trying to rescue it, the transom was covered by the water and the rowboat was sinking into the lake. I stood on the shore and tried to watch as it sank but lost sight of it as it plunged toward the darkness at the bottom of the lake. The last thing I saw was the long, tailing white rope as it dragged the spade down into the depths.

There was nothing I could do.

I went home and spent the rest of the night in my tree fort.

That's the story. That's what happened. You asked me about that one summer, and I told you the truth.

You asked what had happened with my friends that summer, and I told you everything.

You asked about that summer when I refused to go outside, and that is why. That is why I stayed in my room reading for most of summer vacation that year.

I know you were worried about me; it's one of the things that made you a great parent. But I didn't want to face the neighbourhood. You often suggested that I invite Andy over to play, or asked if I wanted to ride to Darren's, or take some of your homemade cookies to Jeff Marcella's house. But I always made an excuse to stay home.

I remember once that summer you said it was nice to have me home. Then you asked what I did in my room all day. Mostly I read books, some about basic engineering but mostly about sailing ships.

COUNTRYFEST

BAND PRACTICE.

"The Middle 8's."

May 1987.

The rehearsal space (my parents' basement).

"Great news! We're playing Countryfest!" I said as I walked into the room, followed very closely by Guitar. I gave the other two members of the band, Bass and Drummer, my biggest smile. This was a big deal, no, an enormous deal, especially for a high school garage band that had never even played a paying gig.

I was expecting cheering, at least a round of high-fives, but they just sat and stared. So I repeated myself, more excitedly this time, so that maybe they would realize that this was a big deal, no, an enormous deal. "We're playing Countryfest!"

No cheering. Just a question from Drummer. "How'd you do that?"

"He lied," Guitar said, so loud he was almost shouting. Until that moment, I had not noticed the anger in his eyes, even though he had been sitting beside me during the entire phone call with the booker.

"I never lied," I corrected.

"You told them we had just recorded our second CD!" He was actually shouting now.

"We have. Remember, we made that demo. Well, I thought we should have a backup copy, so I burned a second one. Not a lie. We have recorded our *second* CD."

"You told them we'd been playing together for fifteen years." He sounded even angrier now as he plugged in his guitar and pulled the strap over his head.

"We have." I had the distinct feeling that I was on trial and that Bass and Drummer were the jury.

"We had our first rehearsal like a month ago!" he shouted and began to adjust knobs and switches on his guitar and amp.

"You and I have each been playing for about five years. He's been playing for four years," I said, pointing to Bass. "He got his kit last summer. That's close to a year." I flashed out the numbers on my fingers. "Five years, plus five years, plus four years, plus one year. That's fifteen years *together*."

Guitar threw his hands in the air and walked back to dig something out of his backpack, which he never called a backpack, always his "gig bag."

I was thinking about how I should deliver my closing arguments in the case. Maybe something energizing about how this was going to be our big break. Then Guitar came back at me, throwing his hands up again to show the jury how preposterous he thought my defence was.

"You said that our lead singer was flying in from Nashville for the show!"

I was waving my finger at Guitar before he even finished the accusation. "My family is going there this summer. My cousin is getting married. I'll be back the week before the show. So ... yes ... technically ... our lead singer will be flying in from Nashville for the show."

Guitar gave up and went to sit on his amp. Having lost this case, he decided to charge me with a different crime. "Why did you pick such a stupid name?"

I had no other option. I decided to plead guilty to the lesser charge. "Yeah, sorry, when she asked what we were called, I panicked. I needed a name for a country band, and it was the first country singer I could think of."

"It's stupid," he repeated.

"Yeah, I know," I said.

"What did you say?" said Bass, breaking his silence.

I decided to try to hype it up, try to put a positive spin on my bad decision. "When we play Countryfest this summer," pause to let the excitement set in, "we'll be called ... DRAMATIC PAUSE ... *Willie and the Nelsons*."

"It's stupid," they said in unison.

We never did practice that night. We talked about "the gig" (I know I wasn't the only one who was delighted to be able to use that expression legitimately for the first time) and agreed to meet three days later with some song ideas to play at Countryfest (the gig).

I didn't know much about country music. All I had ever heard was a few scattered seconds as I flipped past the country station on the radio. Luckily, I had been forced to take piano lessons. That meant I could get a crash course in old country songs.

My piano teacher was Mrs. Bennett. She was ancient in my mind, probably only sixty at the time, but to a teenager anyone with grey hair is a fossil. She made it very clear that she did not like country music and that I would not be learning to play it with her. But she did agree to let me borrow a book titled *The Great Songbook of Country Music*.

At the next rehearsal, the first one for Willie and the Nelsons, we pored over the songs in the book and discussed which ones we should try to learn. We didn't know any of the songs, so we just looked for titles that were catchy, like "Okie from Muskogee" or ones that had cool lyrics like "wasted time is time well spent" or "the last thing I needed, the first thing this morning."

I insisted on keeping it simple. I automatically vetoed anything I thought would be too hard. See, I was the only one in the band who read music. (That is actually very common. Many of your favourite musicians can't read music.) However, since the book was written for piano, it was up to me to figure out the music, then I had to teach everyone their part of the song. And I had to do it all without having ever heard the songs before. See, we weren't country fans; we didn't own any records. All we had was what was written in *The Great Songbook of Country Music*.

Before long, we had developed a working system, a flawed one but one that worked for us. I would learn the songs on piano, and that would give me the basics. Then I would take that and adjust it for guitar. Then I would divide up the portions that I would play (rhythm) and what Guitar would play, and what Bass and Drummer would play.

There are almost too many flaws in this system to count.

First, many piano-based songs are written in keys that are not commonly used in guitar playing. Also, almost every time, the chords needed to be adjusted depending on what we could play.

The first song we learned is a good example.

I insisted we learn Willie Nelson's song "On the Road Again." I figured if we were going to be stuck with the name Willie and the Nelsons, we should play at least one of his songs, and this was the easiest one in the songbook.

On the piano, the song starts in G, but on the guitar it's E; that was an easy change. But the next chord is G#7. We couldn't play that, so G#7 was changed to G. In all, each change was a small change, but when you added together all the small changes, our song was very different from the original.

The hardest for me was teaching the songs to Bass. Not the chords, but knowing how much the bass player should play. The bass plays a supporting role in the band, working behind the scenes, usually unnoticed by the average listener. They are to the band what the sound engineer is to a movie. Essential, but the audience only notices when they screw up.

That's how we learned each song. I learned it a little bit wrong. Then taught that to the band a little bit wrong. Then we'd play it together a little bit wrong.

However, since none of us had heard these songs, we had no idea how wrong we were. We were headed to a disaster, but we had no idea.

Before long, we had a bunch of songs from *The Great Songbook of Country Music*. When we weren't rehearsing, we were still always talking about "the gig" (man, I loved saying that). We talked about what songs sounded best and which ones seemed to fit together. Eventually, we had a solid setlist.

We decided that it made sense to open with a Willie Nelson song, and since we only knew one, it made the choice easy. After "On the Road Again," we'd jump right into "Thank God I'm a Country Boy" by John Denver. Then I had scripted a quick introduction of the band, after which we started playing "Okie from Muskogee" by Merle Haggard. Then we'd slow things down for a pair of songs, "Your Cheatin' Heart" and "The Gambler." Again, we'd never heard the songs before, but we agreed that the lyrics were great and, probably most importantly, they were chords we knew how to play.

Our best song was a really old one, and it was our best because it was the only one we had a recording of. The songbook said it was written in 1963 by Buck Owens and was titled "Act Naturally." We knew it as a song by The Beatles. Guitar brought in his dad's copy of the album

Help!, and we listened to it over and over again till we had it down pat.

If you don't remember that song on the album, don't sweat it. You wouldn't be the only one who missed it. It was a "Ringo song," after all. See, Ringo Starr was initially the most popular member of the band. Seriously. Ringo was already an established musician, and he was a really cool-looking guy, so he had fans of his own even before he joined The Beatles. So management decided to have him sing lead on a few songs to capitalize on that popularity. You still don't believe that Ringo was more popular than John or Paul, but it's true. The Beatles would add songs to their set list specifically to get him out from behind the drum kit and singing at the front of the stage. But the song had to be something that Ringo could sing, and it was usually an old song that he felt comfortable with. Thus, the old country song "Act Naturally" became a "Ringo song."

So, for us it didn't matter if it was a very old and obscure song that was added to the album because fans liked the drummer. Finding a recording of this "Ringo song" meant we could learn it correctly. Since we knew that this was the only song we were assured to be playing correctly, we decided, in the hope of leaving the stage on a high note, we would finish our set with it.

Our drummer never sang. It was enough to task him with keeping the beat, keeping the rest of the band in time. That's the drummer's primary job. Pick your cliché, but the drummer is the backbone, the heartbeat, the engine of the band. They are all those things at once, so they need to be good. But it's even better if they are great.

However, the difference between a good drummer and a great drummer is something only other musicians can understand.

Think of it like painting a portrait. If the painting looks like the person, that's a good painter. If the painting looks like it is about to jump off the canvas, if it's so life-like that you half-expect the subject to step through the frame and into the room, that is a great painter. Our drummer, well, if they were a painter you'd look at the portrait and say, "Who is it?" and they would tell you, and then you'd say, "Oh yeah, I can see it now."

Rehearsals went by, the summer was almost over, and Countryfest was just around the corner. My family flew to the wedding in Nashville. My mom kept telling relatives about the upcoming concert. It was my first taste of attention as a musician. I loved it.

When we came back, the summer was almost over, and Countryfest was around the corner.

We felt we were ready.

We weren't.

But we didn't know it.

I remember going to bed the night before, thinking about how perfect the show was going to go. I had borrowed the family minivan for the trip. The route to the show was mapped out, and we were even leaving two hours early, in case. Each of us had already packed our extra gear. Everyone had extra strings, picks, sticks, and cables, just in case. We had even practiced loading the minivan to ensure everything would fit. Everyone chipped in for gas, and my mom had packed us a cooler full of snacks, sandwiches, and water. Drummer's kit was already in the minivan, since it took so long to load. I fell asleep relaxed and confident that we were ready.

Then disaster struck.

This I couldn't have expected.

I couldn't have anticipated that while I slept, we were losing our drummer.

Heck, I didn't even know there was an election.

Guitar was at my house thirty minutes early, but I had been standing in the driveway for twenty minutes before that. He walked around the corner at the end of my block, looking every bit like the lead guitarist he wanted to be. He wasn't walking to ride in a borrowed minivan; he was strutting to a gig.

Traditionally, the lead guitarist plays the most difficult parts of the song. If you don't believe me, ask a lead guitarist.

They are the mirror image of the rhythm guitar, the part I played, maybe too well. See, rhythm guitar has a role to play in everything. They help the drummer provide the steady pulse of a song. They help the bass pull off chord changes. They layer the right chords behind a lead guitarist's riffs and solos. Plus, in my case, they transpose music, book shows, schedule practice, and drive the minivan. Oh, and I had to sing too.

We headed off and picked up Bass and his equipment, just a hard case for his instrument and cables, and headed to Drummer's place. At the door, his father explained that Drummer was working. We knew that Drummer had taken a one-day job. He was supposed to be done last night, but according to Drummer's dad, there was an issue with the ballots, and he couldn't leave.

I heard the words his dad said, but nothing registered in my head. I lied to Drummer's dad, told him that I understood, and asked where he was working so that he could "wish us luck before we left for the gig." This time I didn't like saying that word. It sounded stupid in front of a grown-up.

I told Guitar and Bass that Drummer was stuck at work and that we needed to pick him up. I drove to the polling station; I made no mention of him missing our show. We couldn't play without a drummer, and it was too late to replace him. He would have to come with us.

When we arrived, I told the guys to stay in the mini-van. Bass stayed behind, but Guitar insisted on coming with me. I think he knew I was hiding something.

The front door of the polling station was locked, but I knocked, louder and louder, until an unhappy and official-looking man walked up to the window in the door. I pointed down to the handle, thinking for some reason that he didn't know how to open a door. But he just shook his head and shouted, "The door stays closed until the count is finished."

I tried not to panic as the reality of what was happening seeped in. I smiled and shouted, "We're in Drummer's band. We've got a show in a few hours." He didn't react, so I decided to play my biggest card. "We're playing Countryfest." I guess I thought he would say something like, "You're playing Countryfest! Why didn't you say so! To heck with democracy, you guys are playing

Countryfest!" Of course, he didn't say that. He turned away, saying, "The door stays closed until the count is finished."

My feet were moving me around the side of the low building without any idea of where I was going or what I was planning to do. I started checking in windows as Guitar asked me questions I had no answer to. "What are we going to do?" "Where are we going to get a drummer?" "What if we don't have a drummer?"

I didn't get a chance to answer "I don't know" three times before I saw Drummer in a small room filled with piles of paper and a group of unhappy adults counting in silence. I banged on the window, and Drummer turned around. When he walked to the window, I stepped back to make room. In my mind, this was a rescue operation. He was going to climb out the window and run to jump in the minivan, and we'd peel out of the parking lot as we headed off to freedom. But he never even opened the window.

"I'm sorry, guys, I was going to call, but we were here so late, and then we had to be back first thing. Sorry."

"But we're playing Countryfest!" It was my best card.

"I know. I'm sorry. But the counting machine messed up, and now we have to count every ballot by hand. I'm sorry."

"But we're playing Countryfest!" It was my only card.

"I have to stay." The way he was talking reminded me of how my dad talked when I was getting in trouble for my grades. "I'm the deputy returning officer. This is serious. I have responsibilities," he said, walked back to the table covered in ballots, and sat with the other grown-ups.

We walked slowly back toward the vehicle. Guitar was no longer asking questions; he had decided to instead state the obvious. "We can't do this without a drummer."

I didn't answer.

"They won't let us on the stage without a drummer," he said.

I didn't answer.

"There is no such thing as a band without a drummer," he said.

This I had an answer for. "Sure there are, lots of them. Basically every bluegrass band."

"What are you talking about?"

"The Foggy Mountain Boys, The Country Gentlemen. All the biggest bluegrass bands never have a drummer."

"Okay." He conceded my point, but he wasn't about to lose the game. "Every band *that anyone has ever heard of* has a drummer."

"You've heard of The Righteous Brothers." I shouldn't have, but I poked him in the chest. "You've heard of Simon and Garfunkel." I poked him in the chest again. I really shouldn't have done it a second time. "Neither of them have drummers."

We stopped beside the minivan doors.

"Those are duos. We're a quartet." He was steaming.

"Actually, we're a trio," I said and climbed into the driver's seat of my family's minivan.

We drove to the gig in silence. There was nothing to say.

We just rolled along. After about an hour, Guitar said something that he must have been thinking about for a while, but honestly, it had never occurred to me.

"We could just turn around and go home." He tried to say it gently, like when a parent says to a child, "You tried your best."

I was shocked. "No way. We just need to figure this out. We'll think of something."

"They will never even miss us. Let's just go home." He was defeated.

"No. We're going to play Countryfest. We just need …"

It was at this moment that Bass decided to interrupt and inform us of another disaster.

"Guys, I think I forgot my bass."

"How do you *think* you forgot your bass?" I was shouting. All my anger at Drummer and Guitar was quickly misdirected at Bass.

"I *saw* you put the case in the back," said Guitar. He was shouting now too. More misdirected anger.

"That's the thing," Bass said. "I had everything packed and at the front door, and I was waiting for you guys. Then I decided to take my bass out and go up to my room to practice. Then I went downstairs to grab a snack, and you showed up. So I just grabbed my case and headed out. Now that I think about it, I'm *pretty* sure my bass is sitting in my room."

Guitar put his head down and covered his face. He might actually have been crying. I pulled into the nearest driveway, the parking lot for a Pizza Hut. I parked and ran to the back of the vehicle. The case was empty. No bass. He was right. He had remembered his case with a second strap, extra strings, and lots of cables, but no instrument.

It was over. We were done. Even I had to admit it. We weren't going to be able to play without a drummer *and* a bass player.

There was a very long silence.

Then Guitar spoke. Actually, he shouted.

When he stepped out of the van and yelled, "Hey! Hey you," my first thought was that he was looking for Bass. I thought all that misplaced anger meant Guitar was going to attack him. My second thought was maybe I should let him. But Guitar wasn't looking at us; he was walking away from the minivan and headed across the parking lot to the alley beside the pizza place.

Bass and I didn't know who he was shouting at until we'd caught up with him. It was a guy sleeping beside the Pizza Hut, a little older than us, maybe a lot older than us, wearing jeans and a pair of old boots, long hair tucked behind his ears and a ball cap on top.

Guitar just kept shouting "Hey!" until he was sure that he had the guy's attention, then said, "Can you play drums?"

The guy's eyes were darting all over the place, looking at each of us, staring back at the minivan, surveying the otherwise empty parking lot, then back at us, all in an attempt to figure out why a couple of kids would wake him up by shouting, "Can you play drums?"

He was certainly freaked out, but I wasn't. Surveying random strangers, hoping one of them was a country music drummer, was a terrible idea. But for the first time someone else was being the bandleader. It was nice. Even if we were headed off a cliff, maybe because we *were* headed off a cliff, it was nice to have someone else at the wheel.

Of course, "uh … no" was the answer.

"Can you count to four?" was Guitar's response.

"Y–yyesss," said the guy.

"You're overqualified," said Guitar.

We had a new drummer. Simple as that.

It was just a matter of teaching him to play.

Guitar's idea was actually quite ingenious. He sat in the back with The Guy (we never did ask his name), handed him a pair of sticks, and told him what to hit and when. He laid out the back seat like a drum kit and called out each item in order. The back of my seat was the kick drum, the armrest was the snare drum, the back of the driver's headrest was the ride cymbal, and the cooler my mom had packed was the hi-hat.

Guitar walked The Guy through each song, making each rhythm as simple as possible. He'd say things like, "For this song you're going to play backseat, cooler, armrest, armrest," and once he had the pattern of the song down, they would work on the timing until The Guy had the basic rhythm. Then on to the next song.

Guitar went through each song in the setlist, while in between The Guy ate most of the sandwiches my mom had packed for the trip. He said it had been a long time since he had eaten, and so Guitar just offered him one after another.

I drove and only half listened to the drum lesson. I was too busy driving and navigating. I had mapped out the route months ago. I ticked off the landmarks in my mind as we passed each one: Grindstone Point, Jackfish Lake, the Martin Marina, and finally the exit sign for a tiny community known as Falcon Lake. It is just a cluster of old homes and a golf course wrapped around a lake. But once a year it was transformed to the biggest concert of the summer. And we were the opening band.

The Guy was a natural. By the time I pulled off the highway, The Guy was able to play the basic rhythm for every song in the set. As long as Guitar got him started, he was able to play the same thing for as long as we needed. We didn't have time to cover fancy drum tricks, but he could keep the rest of the band in time, which was good enough, at least for us.

For a moment, just a moment, I thought we might pull it off. Then I remembered an old expression: "If the guitarist makes a mistake, they've made a mistake. If the drummer makes a mistake, then everyone makes a mistake." The drummer keeps the time for the entire band. If they don't do their job, no one else can do theirs. And we were trusting a guy who had just learned to play by beating on the back of my headrest for thirty minutes. Oh, and our bass player still didn't have a bass.

We were doomed.

We got checked in by security, I got my first backstage pass, and we started loading in our gear. The bands that would go on later in the day were all hanging around backstage. I was worried what they would think of our homeless drummer. Wrinkled clothes, long, unkempt hair, worn-out boots, and a dirty baseball cap. Then I realized he looked more like a country musician than anyone else in the band.

We all had clean sneakers and new jeans, short hair and young faces. We were the ones who looked like we didn't belong, mostly because we didn't.

When the roadies went to put our gear on the stage, they also all looked like The Guy. I went backstage trying to borrow a bass from one of the other bands. I asked The Guy to come with me, not that I thought he could help. But I had already lost one drummer today. I wasn't going to let this one out of my sight.

In the area behind the stage, about a dozen guys were sitting around in the large tent backstage marked *Talent*. I felt pretty special walking through the door, knowing that for the first time the word applied to me. Everyone in there was much older than me and had long hair, old boots, and faded T-shirts. The sign might have said that I belonged, but I could see in their eyes that the "talent" did not feel the same way.

I told the group that the "airline" had lost some of our luggage and that we needed to borrow a bass, just for today. No one even spoke. They all just stared, like they were just waiting for me to leave.

Then The Guy stepped up.

"Well, if no one can help us out," he said to me but loud enough to be overheard by everyone. "Let's just take this somewhere else and enjoy it." Then he lifted up the cooler he had carried in from the minivan and tapped the side of the container.

I had no idea what he was doing. He had already eaten all the sandwiches during his "drum lessons." All that was left were a few of my mom's cookies and some bottled water. So when he turned to leave the tent, I just stood frozen in place.

It was a guy sitting at a card table who took the bait. "Now, hold on," he said, putting his cards face down on the table. "I got a bass you can borrow."

"Really? Thanks," I said, still clueless.

Then the old man at the card table got up and strolled over to The Guy. The card-playing musician, who had very long hair, very old boots, and a very faded T-shirt, never even looked at me. He moved around me, like you would step around a chair left inconveniently in the middle of the room, to talk to The Guy. The card-playing musician smiled, apparently happy to be speaking with one of his kind of people, and said, "A bass for a cooler, sounds like a fair trade."

"Yep, that's fair," The Guy replied and shook the card player's hand. He led us to the large tour bus that housed his band's gear and popped the door to one of the luggage compartments under the bus. I noticed that the door wasn't locked. It struck me as odd that he would keep a precious musical instrument in an unlocked cargo compartment.

When he pulled out the bass, I realized my error. This was no precious item, no backup instrument — this was a forgotten reject, and its best parts had been harvested for better instruments.

Any bass I have ever seen had two sets of coils called pickups. This one had just one; there was a gaping hole where the second one used to be. It had been removed, most likely to fix a better instrument. This bass was covered in so many scratches and chips that it was hard to tell the original colour.

This was not a benchwarmer waiting to go into the game. It was a treasure chest with nothing in it. It was a rusted car sitting on blocks in a farmer's field. Once it may have been something special, but now it was just this side of useless.

Oh, and it had no strings too.

"I never said it was pretty," the card-playing musician said pointedly, "and with the single coil, you gotta watch out for buzzing. Ah, I don't got strings for it, either. But a deal's a deal." Then he reached out a hand for the cooler.

We exchanged items.

Looking back, it was actually a fair deal. We got a very disappointing bass and he got a cooler that he would soon be very disappointed to find had no beer inside.

To my surprise, Bass was delighted to see us return with what I would barely call "a musical instrument." He quickly strung the instrument backstage. I was silently thankful that he had at least remembered to bring extra strings.

But just a little behind schedule.

With a drummer who had never actually played drums.

A borrowed bass would need a lot of work to be considered garbage.

A playlist of songs that were about to play wrong.

Willie and the Nelsons went on stage at Countryfest.

The local radio DJ who was supposed to introduce us was nowhere to be found, so without any build-up or fanfare or even an intro, we walked onto the stage as the first performers of the weekend. I had been thinking about this moment for months and had pictured it in a thousand different ways. But in all the pictures I had drawn in my head, there was always an audience.

When I walked onto the stage and waved to the crowd, just like I had practiced in my imagination, there was no one. As I adjusted the microphone, I surveyed the "crowd."

Directly in front of the stage was a huge empty area of grass. The space looked even bigger, since not a single person was standing there. Far off to my left were the concession stands and a long line of portable toilets. Well off to the right side of the stage was a surprisingly big crowd already in line for beer. I say "surprisingly big" because there were about forty or fifty people in line, and the beer tent had only been open for about three minutes.

Way at the back on a hill was the sound booth, where a lone technician stood giving me the thumbs-up. I realized that the tech had seen me waving, and since there was no audience, he assumed I was waving at him.

He waved back.

I stopped waving.

I thought that the sound guy was the only person who was going to hear us play, and maybe it was a good thing.

As Willie and the Nelsons, we had agreed to start with "On the Road Again." As the rhythm guitarist, I was the one who started the song. It's a simple rhythm that's fun to play. The intro is just a bouncy series of E chords until the vocals start.

I started with the intro, but because of my nerves, it was a little too quick. But I reminded myself that I would only be playing alone for two bars, then the drummer (along with the rest of the band) would step in, and I could relax and match his count.

An eight-count later, terror slowly rolled from the top of my head to my feet. I realized that Drummer was hours away, counting ballots. The Guy behind me was waiting for me to start the lyrics. That's how they had rehearsed it in the minivan. To try to keep it simple, the opening lyric was his cue to start playing "armrest-cooler-back of the seat." In a flash, I realized that the whole band was waiting for me to start singing.

Then I forgot all the words.

Yes, the opening line of the song "On the Road Again" is "on the road again."

Yes, most of the lines of the song "On the Road Again" are "on the road again."

I know that now, but at the time I was too panicked to remember. But I had to say something. So I introduced the band. I kept playing the bouncy intro and said to no one at all, "Good morning everyone, we're Willie and the Nelsons. We are delighted to be here to kick off Countryfest. It is my pleasure to introduce the band to you." I looked over at Guitar with a smile that I hoped said, "Just go with it." He looked back at me with a smile that said, "What are you doing?" I made a big deal of introducing each member of the band, even pausing after each name for the applause that never came, from an audience that wasn't there.

When I got to the drummer, since I didn't know his name, I just said, "And on drums, well, he's a true man of mystery. And if you know him, you know everyone just calls him The Guy." I heard Guitar laugh beside me, and it broke the tension. I got a little closer to the mic and was about to start the lyrics I had finally remembered when I did something we had never practiced: I dedicated a song.

There was a guy near the back of the line-up for the beer tent. He looked a lot like our new drummer. And by that, I mean he may also have slept in the alley beside a pizza place last night. He was wearing a faded Willie Nelson concert T-shirt and a custom-made hat that read "Wild Bill." I talked into the side of the mic to turn my focus directly at Wild Bill, who was very much focused on how slowly the beer line was moving. Then I said, "This one goes out to Wild Bill. We know you'll enjoy this one as much as we do."

Wild Bill looked toward the stage and smiled in surprise. I ended the extremely long intro and started to sing. The rest of the band, including the drummer, kicked in right on cue, and we were off.

Something clicked with Wild Bill. Maybe it was because we dedicated the song to him. Maybe it was because we were playing a song he loved. Maybe it was because we were playing it almost twice as fast as we should. Maybe it had something to do with the flask in the back pocket of his jeans. But whatever it was, he was instantly a fan.

Our first.

By the time we got to the second verse, he was already dancing at the end of the beer line. Before the end of the chorus, he was dancing from picnic table to picnic table and getting the beer tent patrons to sing along. When we reached the fourth verse, which should have been the end of the song, he just kept dancing, I just kept singing, and the band just kept playing.

Much like our flawed plan to start the song, we had a flawed plan when it came to ending it. The Guy was waiting for Bass to tell him when to end the song. Bass was supposed to yell to him when were at the chorus for the last time. Then after I sang the last "and I can't wait to get on the road again," The Guy was supposed to count out four beats and then hit the ride cymbal (the back of the driver's headrest) three times. But Bass forgot; it was something he never had to do before, and it most likely got lost with all the "first gig" nerves, so we just kept playing.

But Wild Bill didn't seem to mind. Before we were halfway through the song for the second time, he was swinging arm-in-arm with strangers in the beer line. It was like he was at an out-of-control square dance. He'd link elbows with a dance partner, spin them around in a circle a few times, then let go and move on to the next closest person and do the same to them. As he let each new dance partner go, he'd fling them out of the beer tent area and out toward the empty patch of lawn in front of the stage. With each reluctant dance partner, Wild Bill would spin a little faster and fling them a little farther. Before we were about to get to the end of the song, for the third time, he was leading the entire beer tent audience in a sing-along and had moved half of the line-up onto the grass in front of the stage.

As we neared the end of our fourth time through the song, I turned and nodded at Bass, who clued in and turned to The Guy and told him it was time to end the song. After my last "on the road again," the whole band turned to the drummer and followed his lead as we played the end and finished the song for good.

The crowd, which was still small but was much larger than nothing, cheered. We had played our first song at Countryfest, and the audience was cheering. It was amazing. I didn't want the feeling to end. Everything had been worth it. The practicing. The lessons. Hauling equipment. Lying to get this gig. Coming here with a drum kit but no drummer and a bassist without a bass had all been worth it. For a few seconds, a handful of strangers clapped for us. It was magic.

We jumped right into our second song, just like we had planned. However, since it had worked so well the first time, I wanted to dedicate it to someone in the crowd. I pointed to a girl about my age, one of the first people that "Wild Bill" had danced with, and said in the deepest voice I could, "This one's for you, darlin'." Then I winked at her and started the clapping that begins "Thank God I'm A Country Boy." It worked perfectly. She was clapping along, and soon so were most of the people at the beer tent picnic tables.

And that is how the rest of Countryfest went for Willie and the Nelsons. I'd dedicate a song to someone in the audience. We'd play it, slightly wrong and much too fast. Then do it again. Before I knew it, we had played all our songs. We finished strong with the Buck Owens/Ringo Starr song, and the set was over.

I can still remember the exact sound of those people clapping as we jogged off the stage.

Were we discovered that day and went off to fame and fortune? Of course not.

Was it a flawless demonstration of musicianship? Nope.

Were we even playing the songs right? Technically, no.

Was it the best show we had played? Honestly, no.

But we had played Countryfest, and that's the truth.

THE BRAVE KNIGHT AND
THE DISTANT OUTPOST

THERE ONCE WAS A BRAVE knight. Having been given a quest by the king, he headed off to the most distant outpost in the kingdom. This outpost lay on the very edge of the kingdom and was situated closest to the border of the kingdom's sworn enemy. There had been peace with the enemy, mostly due to two important factors. One, the king insisted that the soldiers stationed on this distant outpost maintain a constant vigil along its wall to watch for any sign of trouble. Two, past the distant outpost and separating it from the kingdom of the enemy was a deep, dark forest.

This deep, dark forest was believed to be home to a host of horrific monsters: savage beasts that hunted in the darkness of the woods, slithering nightmares that waited for their prey in the undergrowth, flying killers with silent wings that lurked in the shadows of the forest canopy.

For many years, the distant outpost and the deep, dark forest that lay on its doorstep had been silent. Until now.

Each week, the soldier who had served the longest at the outpost was sent on the long journey back to the king's court, carrying official dispatches from the outpost commander to the king. Another soldier was then sent to take his place at the outpost. Since the outpost held a small garrison of ten, this meant that each soldier was only stationed at the remote location for ten weeks from the time they were sent to the outpost to the time they were sent back to the king's court.

As the king commanded, the soldiers stationed at the outpost maintained a constant vigilant watch on the wall of the small camp. This is what the brave knight expected to see when he finally approached the outpost. Instead, he saw just the deep, dark forest.

After three full days of riding, he had anticipated seeing the distant walls of the outpost and the soldiers who walked those walls day and night. But as the third day came to an end, he saw only forest. The deep, dark forest that should still have been a full day's ride past the outpost. He paused for a moment, wondering if he had somehow gotten lost. But he was headed in the right direction, and the outpost was in the same location as always. But the forest had grown and now surrounded the outpost.

Confident that he was well-armed and well-trained, he decided to continue the way he was headed and risk entering the forest that he, and everyone else in the kingdom, believed to hide deadly horrors.

Before long, he saw the image of the remote outpost in the distance, just as the sun set behind him and the sky beyond the forest turned from orange to red. As he neared the outpost, the brave knight saw what he feared more than any legend of any monster in the deep, dark forest: the walls of the outpost were empty.

The knight spurred his horse and quickened his pace to the gates. He knew from his briefing by the king that the outpost had just one entrance, a huge wooden door that could only be opened from the inside. If everyone in the outpost were dead from a plague or illness, as the knight began to fear, he would have a very difficult time getting inside to safety before nightfall.

The outpost was little more than a group of wooden buildings surrounded by a high stone wall. In each of the four corners of the compound lay a building: a barracks where the men would sleep when not on duty, an armoury where a large number of weapons were stored in case of attack, a kitchen that also served as a dining hall, and the captain's quarters that housed the outpost's commander. The massive stone wall that enclosed the outpost even encompassed the single door into the compound, allowing the men on guard to walk around the entire fortified area. This wall, just wide enough for two men to pass each other while atop, had been built to withstand almost any attack.

The wall was smooth stone. Near the top, the angle of the wall was built to lean out toward the forest, making climbing it all but impossible. As the knight moved in closer to the outpost, he still saw no signs of life and wondered if it had been taken by force. However, there were no signs of warfare. There were no burned buildings in the compound, no ladders leading up the wall, and no enemy soldiers dead outside the wall. Even the outpost's single door seemed to be securely shut. As far as the knight could tell, the only sign that anything was wrong was the forest. That was supposed to be miles away and now reached the very walls.

The brave knight brought his horse to a stop in front of the outpost's large single door when something hit him square in the chest. It knocked the wind out of his lungs and made him gasp as the offending object fell to the ground beside his horse. It was a table leg.

He stared at it for a moment, seeing it lying there, not realizing it had been thrown from the top of the outpost wall until he heard a confusing call. "You're real. You're real. I didn't believe it, but you're real. Oh, I'm sorry, I'm sorry I hit you. I'll be right down to let you in. You're real."

The voice was that of a young boy. To the knight, he looked far too young to be a soldier. While the knight stretched and recovered his breath, he heard the grating sounds of iron and wood that meant that the outpost door was opening.

Before the door was open more than a crack, a young boy stepped out and ran to take the reins of the knight's horse. The boy was breathless as he continued to confuse the knight with apologies and ramblings. "I had to be sure you were real. I'm sorry. We need to get inside. It's getting late. We need to get inside. I am sorry that I hit you, but I am glad that you're here and that you're real."

The boy would not listen to any of the knight's questions. "Who are you? Where is the outpost commander? What happened here? What do you mean when you say you needed to see if I was real?"

The boy ignored him, something the knight was not used to, and instead all but dragged the knight from his horse, leaving it in the courtyard just inside the gate. Only after he had secured the gate and closed himself and the knight inside the barracks would the boy answer the knight, and this is what he told him.

To no surprise, the boy had lied about his age to serve in the king's army. He had been stationed at the distant outpost immediately. On his second day at the outpost, the three men who made up the morning patrol did not return. The commander had tasked two of his veteran soldiers to find them, but they also failed to return. By the time the sun had set, the outpost commander ordered the gate closed and the three remaining men, the commander, and the boy to walk the walls throughout the night.

The commander made a point of explaining to the young boy that patrols had gotten lost before, and he fully expected to see both patrols return the next morning. The commander did not seem worried, which the boy admitted comforted him greatly. However, the next morning the missing soldiers did not return. But even more concerning was that as the sun rose the commander saw that the outpost was now surrounded by trees. The day before, the forest had been but a distant sight on the horizon, but the commander now saw that overnight the deep, dark forest had grown to touch the very walls of his outpost.

The commander immediately ordered that no patrols go out and told the men that he believed they would soon be under attack. The men were ordered to maintain their vigilance on the walls, but as the day passed, no attack came. The soldiers continued to walk the walls, even taking their meals and brief rests there, but no danger was seen until the day was over.

The boy explained that it seemed the sun set with an unnatural speed, the colours of the sunset racing from yellow to pink to red. But before the last rays could fade in the west, the boy saw one of the older men reach for an arrow and aim over the wall of the outpost. Almost as soon as he let the arrow loose, the old soldier turned to the boy and said, "I hit it." The boy looked to where the man had been aiming to see a huge deer staggering off into the woods. It was a beautiful buck with giant antlers and the old soldier's arrow lodged in its right leg. The deer was slowly limping away into the growing darkness of the forest.

The boy tried to stop the old man, but he insisted on following the deer. "I need to track it," he said desperately. "I have to be quick, or I won't be able to find it." The old man slung his bow onto his shoulder and began to climb over the wall. "I've seen this before when hunting with my sons. It may be wounded, but it can still move quickly. I have to follow it, or I will lose it in the forest. My sons are going to be so proud when they see the feast their father is bringing home," the man said as he scrambled over the wall and climbed down the branches of a huge pine next to the outpost wall.

A tree that had not been there the day before.

The boy immediately went to the outpost commander and reported what had happened. The commander ran to the wall and called for the old soldier to return. As soon as the man stepped into one of the growing shadows in the forest, he began to scream. It was not a scream of fear — it was a scream of pain. It was filled with agony, and it was still echoing through the forest as the last sliver of the sun dropped behind the horizon.

Soon after, the commander ordered the braziers, which normally lit the outpost courtyard, to be moved to the outpost walls. He agreed with the other soldiers that the fires would make them more visible, but it was the only way to see if anything was approaching in the darkness.

As the night wore on, the braziers were lit and the commander ordered each soldier to be stationed on one of the four walls. That way there would be at least one person looking in each direction, giving them the best chance of seeing the approaching enemy. As the boy paced back and forth along his portion of the wall, he noticed the man stationed closest to him was speaking to him as if they were already engaged in conversation.

"Yes, she will be very worried, you're right. I was supposed to be home weeks ago, and we were to be married two days ago," he muttered. The boy was about to ask the other soldier what he was talking about when the man stood up from his place on the wall and started shouting. "Abby, my love, you came for me. These woods are dangerous. Quickly, come inside."

Then the man quickly descended the ladder that went down from the wall to the ground inside the compound.

The commander and the other soldiers scrambled after him, but the man was too quick. He was out the gate before the men could intercept him. Unable to stop him and fearing for their safety, the commander closed and locked the gate behind the fleeing man.

As the only one left on the wall, the boy alone saw what happened. As the man ran into the darkness of the woods, the boy looked to see where he was headed. Then he saw her: a beautiful maiden in a wedding dress.

Her dress and veil were both long and white, and she wore a crown of yellow flowers in her hair. She was smiling and waving to the man. The boy thought that she did not look like a person who had travelled for three days in the wilderness. She was happy and clean. She looked like a memory or a dream.

When the soldier approached his lady love, she began to fade, turning to smoke as he reached for her. He watched in stunned silence as the image of his betrothed blew away in the wind. The boy yelled for the soldier to run, but his voice was drowned out by the man's screams. There were no words, just the sound of pain. The boy covered his ears and closed his eyes and began to wish silently that the man would stop screaming. The boy admitted to the knight that he made that wish several times before the wailing finally stopped.

After scrambling up to the boy and hearing the tale of what had happened, the commander declared that no one was to leave the outpost for any reason until sunrise.

With just the boy, the commander, and one other soldier left on the wall, the commander ordered that no one was to guard a post. Instead, they would walk the wall constantly for the rest of the night.

After many hours of silence, the boy spotted something in the gloom. As it moved into the pale light cast on the wall by the brazier, the boy began to see that it was an old man. He was dressed in merchant clothes and carried a small, locked chest. The boy was about to call out to him and warn him of the danger of being in the forest at night when the other soldier put his hand on the boy's shoulder. "Look, he's wounded," the soldier said, and the boy realized that the merchant had a large slash across his belly that was bleeding badly. The boy was surprised he had not noticed the wound before.

Then the old merchant collapsed, and when he fell, the chest he was holding broke open. Diamonds and jewels tumbled out and spilled onto the forest floor. The other soldier moved to place his right foot on the top of the outpost wall as if planning to jump down.

"Wait," the boy said, "we must tell the commander."

The other soldier grabbed the boy's face, covering his mouth and squeezing his checks. "Why?" he asked. "So he can claim it for himself? So he can confiscate it in the name of the king and leave nothing for us? No. I will grab the chest. You can lower down a rope for me, and we will split it. Just the two of us." The soldier stepped up on the wall of the outpost and turned back to the boy, saying, "Look at the ground, the landing is soft. I will be back before the commander even knows I am gone."

Before the boy could respond, the man leapt from the wall. As soon as he did, the image of the merchant and the chest he was carrying turned to smoke. When the soldier hit the ground, the boy heard a loud crack, followed immediately by screaming. The boy knew that all he could do was pray for the screaming to be short, and it was. The man's final gurgling noise was over by the time the commander made it to where the boy stood with his eyes closed and his hands over his ears.

The commander listened as the boy told him what had happened and declared that for the rest of the night they would walk the wall of the outpost together.

The boy lost track of how many times he and the commander had circled the outpost, just the two of them walking in silence, peering out in the deep darkness that surrounded them. Then, eventually, the braziers began to die down.

The commander told the boy to head down to the floor of the compound and tie a rope around a pile of firewood, then use the rope to pull up the firewood. This would allow the commander to remain on patrol on the wall.

When the wood was loaded, the boy climbed to the top of the wall and found the commander staring into the darkness, watching a man approach in the distance. The man was dressed in the uniform of a high-ranking commander from the enemy kingdom. He was approaching slowly and carrying a white flag. As the boy reached him, the commander began to shout and climb down the ladder from the wall. "They are surrendering! It is over, and we have won! This cursed night is finally over." The boy was unable to stop him from leaving the fort and watched helplessly as the surrendering man turned to smoke. The boy did not want to be thought of as a coward, but he admitted to the knight that he looked away before the screaming even began and wept long after it ended, still able to hear the final sounds in his mind — the sound of breaking bones, the sound of splashing wetness on the forest floor, and the sound of choked cries for help.

The boy was then alone at the outpost. And as expected, the illusions began almost immediately. He had resumed the march along the outpost wall and had only completed the circle once when he saw him. It was his father, smiling and beckoning to him, saying that he had come to rescue the boy from the outpost and that his family was worried sick.

The boy explained to the knight that he knew it was a mirage. He said that his father was a fiend; he would never come looking for the boy. No one in his family had ever been worried about his safety, although he admitted that what he desired most was for a loving parent to come rescue him. The knight realized at that moment that this boy was different from other young men who lied about their age to join the army. They joined seeking excitement and glory; this boy had joined to escape a life of neglect and violence.

When the boy shouted for the image of his father to leave, it started to silently approach the wall of the outpost. Unsure what to do, the boy notched an arrow and shot it into the woods. Just as the arrow was about to strike the mirage of his father, the image turned to smoke and vanished.

As the long night continued, the boy was beset by all manner of illusions: his mother and his siblings; servants carrying platters heaped with food; even the school headmaster, who demanded that he return immediately to his studies. Each time one of these images appeared, the boy shot an arrow at the illusion and watched as it turned to smoke before it was hit. As the night wore on, the boy grew exhausted with fatigue and fright. It seemed to him that new images began to appear almost as soon as the old ones turned to smoke.

The exhausted boy shot more and more arrows into the woods. Many found their target, but most missed and simply vanished into the darkness of the woods or stuck in nearby trees. Before the braziers burned down again, the boy had shot every arrow over the walls at the attacking illusions. Before he saw the first rays of the rising sun, he had thrown every spear over the walls. Before the sun was up and the boy finally allowed himself to rest, he had thrown everything he could gather over the outpost walls. When he saw the knight approaching at the beginning of the next evening, all he had left to throw was the table leg from the commander's quarters.

Having heard the boy's tale, the knight comforted him. "You have acted bravely in defence of this outpost, and when we return I will tell the king of your courage and see that you are promoted and rewarded. But for now, you will sleep in your own bed tonight. I will walk these walls and keep you safe. I will not be tempted, and I have many arrows with me to repel any attackers." The knight smiled at the boy and sent him to the barracks to sleep, then he stocked the braziers on the walls for the long night ahead.

The knight was not on the wall by himself very long before he saw it. In truth, he heard it first. It was so large that as it moved through the dense forest it couldn't help but make a lot of noise, pushing branches out of the way and breaking twigs on the forest floor. The knight knew exactly where it would emerge from the darkness of the trees, but it was much bigger than expected. It was a huge black bear, bigger than any he had ever seen. His first thought was that it would make the perfect trophy. Its fur would be a warm thick blanket, and its head would be mounted on the wall above his fireplace, impressing everyone who entered his home. The knight was reaching for an arrow when he thought that the bear was impressive enough that it could be a gift for the king himself. This made him smile.

He put the arrow back in its quiver. He would need to be more careful with his thoughts. He could not blame himself for seeing and hearing the giant bear. There was obviously a powerful magic overpowering his senses. He was, however, responsible for letting his imagination run wild. As the knight stared down at the bear, he watched it turn to smoke and disappear. He swore to be more careful if he should see anything else.

It did not take long. As the knight continued with his patrol, he saw a man pulling a wagon.

Dressed in fine clothes and wearing the badge of a tax collector, the man was pulling a two-wheeled cart loaded with several large chests. As the man laboured to pull the heavy wagon up a small hill, the knight saw him turn pale and collapse face-down on the ground. As he did, one of the wheels broke off the cart and the chests crashed to the ground, spilling huge piles of gold coins. The tax collector was clearly dead, and the knight could see that it would be very simple to repair the cart and head off with its precious cargo.

He started to laugh. "You must be truly out of ideas if that is the best you can conjure," he shouted into the darkness. "Enough of this pointless game," he commanded the forest and resumed his walk along the wall. If the knight had turned back, he would have seen the man, the cart, and the chests disappear into smoke.

Hours ticked by in silence, and the knight thought he had gotten his wish and the game had come to an end. Then, just before dawn, he saw banners flapping high in the air. The white-and-blue banners were waving gently in the breeze as riders carried them toward the outpost. Within seconds, the knight could see the horses leading the procession. First came the standard bearers and then the scouts on their swift steeds. Next was the outpost commander, followed by the soldiers stationed at this very outpost, who, according to the boy, were all dead. The knight was about to call out to the procession when he saw what followed: a full battalion of his fellow knights riding in perfect unison, and in the middle of the group on his white horse, the king himself.

The king waved to the knight on the outpost wall and called to him. "Well done, my boy. A test worthy of the captain of the castle guard, and you exceeded all expectations." With that the other knights cheered and the banner carriers blasted a greeting on their silver trumpets. Unsure how to respond, the knight yelled down, "Who goes there?"

The king's company halted at his command, then the king answered. "It is I, your king. You know my face and voice as well as you know your own. I put a test before you, and you passed. You showed bravery, loyalty, and a strong mind. Now, let the garrison of the outpost take its place inside, and you will return with me to take up command of the castle guard."

As the king spoke, the boy, who had been awakened by the trumpets, joined the knight on the wall. When he did, the outpost commander addressed him personally. "I'm sorry we had to worry you so, but we thought that because of your age we could not include you in the plan. I am sorry we deceived you." The boy was relieved and smiled to see his commander and the other men he thought had been killed by the forest.

When the commander was finished speaking, the knight withdrew one of the arrows from the quiver he had carried throughout the night and notched it in his bow. The king was quick to respond. "The test has concluded, and the danger has passed. You can lay down your arms and open the gate." The knight continued his motion, drawing back the arrow and aiming down the shaft at the king. "How dare you!" the king bellowed. "I command you to lower your weapon and open this gate immediately." It was a tone that the knight had heard many times while serving the king, and he began to think better about his actions. He lowered the tip of the arrow but did not loose any tension on the string.

The knight knew the king was an eccentric ruler who often had plans and schemes that he shared with no one else. It was also not unusual for him to visit the most distant lands in his kingdoms, seemingly on a whim. Also, while the castle guard was the most prestigious position a knight could achieve, there was no indication of how its leader was chosen. It would not surprise the knight if the king had constructed an elaborate test involving the disappearance of a distant outpost.

Thinking back on the events of the previous evening, the knight adjusted his aim and raised the tip of the arrow to line up with the head of the lead horse. If the procession were an illusion, the arrow would pass harmlessly through the head of the banner carrier's horse. If, however, the king and his entourage were real, only the banner carrier's horse would be killed. While the king would be furious and the knight would never be named head of the castle guard, no one needed to die due to the knight's paranoia.

Watching the knight change to his new target, the king responded, screaming, "Drop that weapon now." Many of his fellow knights reached for their own weapons, pulling crossbows and bolts from their saddlebags to return fire. Others moved between the king and the outpost to shield him from an attack. The lead banner carrier, realizing that the horse he was riding was the knight's new target, spurred his horse sharply and began to ride away from the outpost, begging the knight not to shoot.

The knight was a very good archer, but a moving target is hard to hit. He had originally aimed at the horse's head, but instead, as the arrow flew and the banner carrier rode off into the woods, the knight realized he was about to strike the poor man in the middle of the back.

If the arrow did not kill the man instantly, he would be severely injured. Being so gravely wounded at a distant outpost, far from any of the castle healers, the man would surely suffer a slow and agonizing death. The knight, who had defied an order and attacked the king's procession, would likely be executed before the sun was fully in the sky.

However, as the arrow struck the fleeing man and while the noise of horses and shouting still echoed in the forest, the banner carrier turned to smoke, followed quickly by the scouts, the knights, and then finally the king himself.

The knight and the boy ate together in the small cabin that served as the dining hall and kitchen for the outpost as the knight told the tale of what had happened overnight. When he was done telling the boy about the bear and the tax collector, the knight declared that they would leave the next day as soon as the sun was up. The boy explained that he could not take another night in the outpost and that they should leave immediately, but the knight told him that they could not.

"It is almost midday, and we would not be able to make it out of the forest before nightfall," he said. "We would be trapped in the woods without the protection of these walls. We would never make it on foot." The boy suggested that with the knight's horse bearing them both, they would be able to leave the forest before nightfall. The knight explained that he had considered it but admitted that his horse was too old.

"While it is loyal and legendary in its exploits, the horse cannot bear us both. If I was alone, I could ride out of the forest, but with one of us on foot, we would not make it." He admitted his mistake to the boy. "I should not have brought this horse. I should have chosen a younger mount. I only chose it thinking that this would be our last quest together. When we get back, I shall ask the king to release me from my duties. Then that horse and I will retire to the countryside, where I have bought a modest farm on the shores of what is known as The Lake of the Falcons."

The boy was heartbroken and terrified at the idea of facing another night walking the outpost walls. He got up from the table and headed to get them more water. As the boy walked to the far side of the room, he began to imagine the horrors that might be waiting for him in the darkness of the forest. He believed that if he was faced with another night surrounded by the evil, something from the deep recesses of his mind would lure him out of the outpost, and soon he would be the one screaming in the shadows of the forest floor. He had no choice. Standing behind the knight, he raised a crude wooden chair above his head and with all his strength, brought it crashing down on the knight's head.

Not that the knight heard what he said, but the boy did apologize. "I'm sorry to leave you like this," he said. "But I will not survive another night on these walls. If the evil in the woods does not take me, then madness will. And as you said, your horse is old and can only bear one of us to safety. I am sorry."

Then he left, taking only enough time to saddle the knight's horse. He rode east as fast as the old horse could carry him.

When the knight awoke, it was very late in the day. By the time he searched the outpost and found that his horse and the boy were gone, the sun was beginning to set. While the knight was very brave, he was concerned about another night in the forest. While he had bested the evil in the forest, he knew that a desperate enemy could be a very dangerous one. He dressed his head wound and checked his supply of food and drinking water. He inspected his bow and each of his arrows. He made sure the braziers were well stocked for the long dark night. He was as prepared as he could be.

But the knight need not have worried. The sun fell, and the evening was quiet. As darkness came, the braziers were lit and the knight walked the wall in silence. He listened to distant birds in the night. He peered deeply at the shadows of the forest but neither saw nor heard anything unusual. He thought often of the boy. He was not angry and did not blame the boy for stealing his horse. He was, after all, very young and had shown amazing courage alone on the outpost wall. When the knight returned to the castle, he would not punish the boy. Instead, he would ask the king to release the boy from the army and offer the boy a job on his farm. Then he would be able to mentor the boy and help him grow into a strong and honourable man.

As the sun started to rise, the knight saw him, walking without the horse and limping badly, making his way through the woods toward the outpost. The knight was delighted to see the boy again and ran away from the wall to the top of the ladder to climb down, then stopped.

While the forest had been quiet and the sun was almost up, the knight still had to be cautious. He needed proof.

He turned back to the outpost wall and looked down at the boy, who was in almost the exact place where the knight had last seen him. The boy was leaning on a large tree, trying desperately to walk over a tangle of tree roots, something that was almost impossible since it required putting all of his weight on his badly injured leg. The boy tried to take a large step with his good foot, lost his balance, and stumbled forward on protruding roots. As the boy fell, his injured ankle was snagged under a thick root and twisted beneath him. The knight heard a loud snap as the boy fell. Fainting from the pain, the young boy collapsed, his head leaned against the trunk of the tree, his injured leg folded beneath him at a painful angle, and his good leg splayed out on the forest floor.

The knight needed to act quickly. If the boy was real, he desperately needed the knight's help. While the knight could wait a few more minutes until the sun was finished rising, the boy might not have that long. Every second counted. But with the boy unconscious on the ground, there was only one way to know if he was an illusion.

The knight reached for one of his arrows and drew the arrow back on his bow. Pausing, he looked down on the boy who, lying injured on the ground so far away, seemed even smaller and younger than before. From the distant outpost wall, the knight could not even be sure that the boy was still breathing. He had no choice but to shoot.

The knight took careful aim and was an excellent marksman, but no one is perfect. Although he had sighted the boy's injured leg, he watched in horror as the path of his arrow went straight to the boy's chest. The boy came to, gasping as the arrow plunged hard into his chest and looking up at the knight with shock in his eyes before falling backwards, sprawling out on the roots of the tree.

Panicked, the knight scrambled down the ladder, burst through the gates of the outpost, and ran for the boy as quickly as he could. His arrow stuck out of the boy's chest. The knight slid to a halt beside the boy and looked down at his small frame beside the giant tree. Its massive trunk and the cluster of ferns at its base left the boy in a dark shadow, untouched by the first rays of the sun.

As the knight reached down to scoop up the small boy and carry him back to the safety of the outpost, he noticed the other arrow, one from his own quiver with the same shaft and fletching. It was buried halfway into the forest floor, just to the left of the boy's leg, inches from where the knight had been aiming.

He stared in silence for a moment. Looking at the arrow stuck in the ground, he saw how the sunlight glowed off the white wood of the shaft and the goose feathers on the end. Then he watched as the line of sunlight moved along the forest floor from the buried arrow and toward the injured boy. As the sun continued to rise and the light spread, the line that divided day and night continued to move to where the boy lay.

As the line crept along the forest floor, it first reached the toe of the boy's boot, and the boot turned to smoke. Then his foot, then his leg, then his arm. The knight watched as the sunbeams turned the boy to smoke. He noted as each part disappeared, the boy's chest, the arrow and the bloodstain. Everything turned to smoke and vanished in the breeze that crept along the forest floor.

When the boy's body disappeared, all that was left was the arrow buried in the dirt exactly where the knight had aimed it.

The brave knight turned and ran for the safety of the outpost, but bravery was not enough. There were too many shadows between him and the gate. Since the outpost was empty, since the commander, the soldiers, and the boy were all gone, there was no one left to hear his screams.

LEARNING TO SWEAR
IN ITALIAN

I ONLY KNOW ONE WORD in Italian.

It is a "bad" word.

I did not know it before I went to summer camp.

The camp was way up north, a big, sprawling place with dozens of cabins spread around half of a huge lake. That's where it got its name, Camp Falcon Lake.

I was going to be a camp counsellor for the first time. I had been a camper for the previous two summers, then one year as a counsellor-in-training, or CIT. The abbreviation was turned into an acronym and pronounced *sit*. Which, of course, was immediately changed to *zit* by the camp counsellors. I was proud to be a zit. Strange, I know, but to me it was a sign of maturity. But more than just growing up, I was working my way to something important. This was my first real sense of achievement. Being a camp counsellor was a goal that I had set for myself and took effort to achieve. I did a good job as a counsellor-in-training, and the next year I was chosen to be a counsellor. I was confident I was going to do a great job.

Until I was assigned my cabin.

There was a longstanding rule at registration that each camper could pick one person to be in their cabin. The policy came from too many kids not wanting to be separated from their best friend. I always thought one of the best things about going to camp is meeting new people, but I can understand wanting to have someone you already know in your cabin.

It can be intimidating walking into a cabin when you don't know anyone there, especially for a preteen who is away from their family for the first time.

Plus, at camp, life revolves around the people in your cabin. You eat at the same table and sleep in the same room. You play sports as a cabin. At evening activities, usually held in the giant mess hall, you participate as a cabin. You enter the lip-sync contest and the talent show as a cabin. When your best friend is doing all those things in a different cabin, it can make you feel like you're losing your bestie.

So, a long time ago, a rule was made: every camper was allowed to choose one friend to be in their cabin. Simple enough.

But some enterprising campers found this loophole and were able to hand-pick all of their cabin mates. See, if each kid could pick one person, then if the campers coordinated their chosen cabin mates, a group of friends could ensure that they were all together. Like, if Susie wanted her four best friends in her cabin, she would put Monique's name down on the form. Then Monique would put Desiree and then Desiree would put Lily and Lily would put Susie. The circle was completed, and the four best friends would be together. This loophole is how I ended up with "the Italian cabin."

That's what everyone called them.

Officially, we were cabin number seven.

But one look at the names of the kids in my cabin, and the nickname stuck. Almost every one of the last names on my list of twelve campers started with "Del" or "De" and ended with "ella" or "ano." Plus, most of my campers came from the same school. While most cabins had one or two kids from the same school, the majority of the Italian Cabin came from one school, Sacred Heart, a Catholic elementary school in a nice part of town.

None of this worried me. Having a group of friends in a cabin meant I might avoid the awkward getting-to-know-you stage at the beginning of the summer. My only concern was for the outsiders, the few kids who did not come from Sacred Heart. As a counsellor, one of my jobs was to make sure everyone was included and that they felt like part of the group. I expected that to be difficult with an already established clique of preteen boys.

In the end, I didn't need to be worried; all of the campers in the Italian Cabin bonded well and quickly.

Mostly because of the BAD WORDS.

Preteen kids away from their parents for the first time often end up saying things they would never say at home.

Usually a *lot* more.

But at camp, that isn't that big a deal.

As counsellors and CITs, we'd usually just reminded them not to be overheard by the other camp staff, like the head counsellors or the instructors. Also, we'd keep tabs on the REALLY BAD WORDS. There were some words and phrases that no camp counsellor would allow. Those words were usually said when the counsellor was not around. Those words were usually said a *lot* when the counsellor was not around.

But my cabin was different. My campers quickly learned that I didn't speak Italian.

They could use all the Italian BAD WORDS they wanted.

Once the "outsiders" in the cabin learned these words, they were no longer outsiders. They were part of the Italian Cabin.

So I let it happen. Saying BAD WORDS in a language no one else understands is pretty harmless.

Plus it brought the cabin together. They bonded over it. They had their own kind-of-secret language.

So, I let it slide.

But to be clear, I knew what they were doing, even if I didn't understand what the words meant. When someone says a BAD WORD, something that they know they shouldn't, you can tell, especially when it's a young camper. They usually whisper it, or at the very least they avoid saying it to the counsellor directly. If that doesn't give it away, the reaction does. Since the "bad" word is used for effect, you can usually tell what it meant by the reaction it gets. Sometimes literally.

Often, the BAD WORD is used to shock people, sometimes to make them laugh, but usually the reaction the word got would tell me the intention. If you paid attention to the placement of the word in the sentence, you could usually guess what it meant. Something in the dining hall like "what's with these BAD WORD scrambled eggs" would be different than something said during a dodgeball game, like "nice throw, BAD WORD." It was those times when I drew the line.

No, not because the second bad word was worse than the first (I couldn't be sure, but it probably was) but because the second one was directed at someone. I did my best to put a stop to the Italian swear words that were directed at other members of the cabin. Same thing with the girls from the other side of the lake.

I couldn't stop the boys in my cabin from talking about girls; it was the thing they talked about most. As preteen boys, they only ever talked about sports, food, and girls. Sports and food took up about three percent of any conversation. I did intervene if the conversation was ever derogatory, or since I didn't understand any of the Italian BAD WORDS, if I thought it was derogatory. Most of the time when they talked about girls, the focus was on what the other guy should do. While I tried to fall asleep and they whispered to each other from their bunks, they gave each other advice. "You should totally talk to her tomorrow." "You should ask her best friend if she likes anyone." "You should see if she's going to the end-of-camp dance with anyone." It was always advice for someone else. They each pretended to know what to do or say, even though I had never seen a single one of them have a one-on-one conversation with a girl. Still, they were all experts.

So I policed the Italian BAD WORDS that my cabin was using, but most of it was harmless and therefore went unchecked.

However, there was one word.

One I couldn't place. One that didn't come with any hints about what it meant. One that seemed to fit into any sentence and was so common that the listener's reactions never gave away its meaning or its weight.

I began to think of it as "that Italian word."

That Italian word went everywhere with our cabin. At breakfast it was, "*That Italian word*, they don't got waffles today." Or at the swim dock, it was, "The water is really cold today, *that Italian word*." And, of course, while they were talking after lights out, "*That Italian word* from cabin three thinks he's got a shot with Robin? *That Italian word*!" It was everywhere. It was part of how they all talked. They included it in every sentence the same way some people include "um" or "eh."

I didn't say it. Except this one day.

So, the camp had this neat tradition of a "cabin challenge." Pretty simple: as part of the morning announcements one cabin would challenge another cabin. The challenging counsellor would be called up when the head counsellors were finished their list of announcements, and they would be handed the big white and blue megaphone and would explain the challenge.

Usually, it was a sport during free time, one cabin against another in a soccer game or a canoe race, out to the farthest buoy and back to the dock. Sometimes it was a one-on-one challenge, like our best against your best in air hockey.

Whatever the contest was, the wager was always the same.

The losing cabin had to be a "runner" for the winning cabin for one meal.

See, every meal at the camp was served the same way. Big communal dishes were placed on the ledge separating the kitchen from the dining hall. Then someone was appointed to be the "runner." Their job was to bring full dishes to the cabin's table, and when all the eggs or meatloaf or French fries had been eaten, they had to take the empty dishes back to the ledge to be refilled.

Simple.

However, if your cabin lost one of these challenges, your cabin had to be the "runner" for the winning cabin.

More than just an inconvenience, the winning cabin would punish the "runner." The winning table would be sure to empty every platter, pitcher, and bowl as many times as possible, as fast as possible.

Plus the winning table would be sure never to run out of two things at once. They'd be sure to finish the mashed potatoes just before you returned with the second helping of corn on the cob. The winners would do the same thing with the juices as well.

I had done that exact thing in my first year as a camper. We had won a cabin challenge, and the "runner" from the losing cabin brought a pitcher of Kool-Aid to our table. I stood up and chugged the whole pitcher before the "runner" could even step away. I belched and handed back the empty pitcher, saying, "We're all out." The "runner" slumped away to fill the pitcher up again. One of the guys in my cabin called me Kool-Aid Man. I replied with "Oh yeah!" and we roared with laughter.

So, while winning a "cabin challenge" was great, losing one was terrible. Losing meant you missed most of your meal while your former opponents stuffed themselves, laughed, and mocked you the whole time.

Since these challenges were pretty disruptive to meals, the head counsellors took it upon themselves to organize them.

They'd talk with the camp counsellors about who was going to challenge who. The head counsellors wanted to make sure that only one challenge happened each day. Plus, they needed to make sure each cabin was challenged at least once but not more than two or three times a summer. It often happened that if there was a cabin with a bunch of good-looking guys in it, they'd be challenged by three or four of the girls' cabins. Those sorts of things wouldn't fly. Everyone needed a chance to be in on the fun. They'd also decide when the challenges could fit into the schedule. For example, they would want all the lifeguards present if there was a swimming race. If the forecast looked like rain, they would suggest that the challenge be a Ping-Pong tournament. That sort of thing.

So one night toward the end of the summer, just after lights-out, most of the counsellors were hanging around at the basketball court. That was their natural hangout, about halfway between the boys' side and the girls' side. It had good lighting and few mosquitos. There were bleachers for hanging out, and since it was a good distance from both genders' cabins, the camp counsellors didn't have to worry about being spied on by campers during their off hours. Not that we got into too much trouble at the basketball court. We were smart enough to find more private places for things that would get us in hot water.

A note:

If you are a grown-up.

If you're concerned about the campers.

They were fine, probably fine.

None of the counsellors would leave our cabin until everyone was safely tucked in, and then the natural safety systems kicked in. First, they were all tired. The mornings always started early, and the days were busy with stuff like swimming and hiking. By the time they got into bed, most of them were exhausted. Second, it got very cool at night. Not exactly cold, but once you were in a comfy, warm sleeping bag, the cool night air made you just want to stay where you were. And maybe most important, there was not much trouble they could get into. With this age group, the only real concern was boys and girls sneaking over to the other side of the camp. And to do that, Romeo or Juliet would have to walk past the basketball court.

So, the basketball court was the perfect place for us to hang out after lights out. Especially for those of us that loved basketball. We played a pretty regular game of pick-up each night, nothing too serious, but sometimes when the right combination of counsellors were all at the court, it could turn into a good game.

Usually, it was driven by me and Darren, the counsellor from the cabin next to mine. He and I clicked immediately. On the first day of camp, we were both wearing the same basketball shoes, Converse Weapons, in the colours of our favourite teams. Mine were in Boston Celtic green and white, and his were Los Angeles Lakers yellow and purple. Those teams were bitter rivals, and we immediately began talking about our prospective teams and arguing about whose superstar was better. It was my hero, Larry Bird, against his, Magic Johnson. This was of course before Michael Jordan took over the league and made our argument pointless. We were the best of friends from that moment on but still always very competitive.

So when the head counsellors asked about scheduling a cabin challenge for my cabin and Darren's, there was no question about what we'd be doing. We'd be playing basketball, and neither of us intended to lose. However, this could be a delicate thing. See, the point was for the cabin to win together, not win because one person was really good at one sport. And not to lose because one person was really bad at one sport. There was an unwritten rule that in these challenges no one was allowed to "take over," and no one was allowed to be picked on.

In the case of a basketball game, if you had a player who was eight feet tall, you weren't supposed to just have them dunk it every time down the court. At the same time, if the other team had a player who couldn't dribble the ball, you weren't supposed to steal the ball from them. You were supposed to let everyone play and then win as a cabin or lose as a cabin. It's why the counsellors encouraged things like canoe races. In something like a canoe race, it was easy for everyone to participate, regardless of skill or strength, and then win (or lose) as a team.

I knew that Darren and I would be a close match as far as skills went. I also knew that he'd follow the unwritten rules as well. But I also knew he was going to take this game seriously, maybe almost as seriously as me. There was only one thing I could do to make sure my team was as ready as possible.

For our challenge, I picked a free period as far in the future as possible. I had never seen any of my campers play basketball or even heard any of them mention the game. So I figured we would need as much time as possible to prepare. The last possible time we could play would be parents' weekend.

This was the last weekend of the summer. Every camper's family was invited to come up and spend the Saturday at camp. They would arrive just after lunch and leave after dinner, which meant that the parents would not only be there to witness the "cabin challenge," but if my cabin lost, they would witness the humiliation as we were forced to be "runners" for Darren's cabin.

The practices went better than expected. First, they could all dribble, and most of them could shoot. I left the first practice feeling very confident about our chances, mostly because I knew I had something I could work with.

There was enough (I'm hesitant to say talent; let's say ability). There was enough ability amongst my campers that I could coach them to a win.

That was the secret to getting around the "unwritten rule." I wasn't allowed to play my best, but there was no rule — written or otherwise — that said I wasn't allowed to "coach" my best. Then, on game day, I wouldn't have to worry about whether I was playing within the "unwritten rules." I could just call the plays and let my team do the rest.

See, basketball strategy is actually very simple. Even the most complicated plays are just variations on a few basic ideas, and this applies to offence and defence. All I had to do was choose the correct plays. It was going to be my job to simplify everything as much as possible so my campers could understand the plays and be able to execute them. With their limited … ah, ability.

We started with defence. The simplest and probably the first basketball defence ever used is called man-to-man. Just like the name says, each player defends against just one player. The defender's job is to stay between the player they are covering and the basket. Simple as that. I told my cabin to find someone on the opposing team who was their height and try to keep that person from getting any easy shots.

For offence, we were going to use three simple plays, but we'd disguise them

I taught my team the pick-and-roll, the wheel, and the UCLA cut. I'm not going to bore you with the mechanics of each, but I will say this: all of those are simple plays that can result in easy baskets.

Perfect for players with limited ability.

The practices were great. I was really proud of how hard my campers worked to understand and execute my plan. We even spent most of our meals going over the plays. I'd be in the middle of the long table, using the condiments as players on the court.

"Okay, you're the ketchup and you have the ball. You're going to pass the ball, which in this case is the saltshaker, to the tartar sauce on the right side. As soon as you do that, vinegar, pepper, and mayo are going to move to the left, which clears the defenders (fork, spoon, and knife) out of your way. Tartar sauce passes back to ketchup for an easy lay-up."

Now, while the offence was simple enough for my campers to execute, my play-calling had to be complex enough that Darren couldn't decipher our plans. So, here's what I did. Each of the three plays would be associated with a colour, a vehicle, or an animal. If I said a colour, they were to run the pick-and-roll. If I said a type of vehicle, they were to run the wheel (get it, wheel, vehicle?) and if I said an animal, they were to run the UCLA cut.

Pretty simple. And this was made even better by throwing some meaningless words into the play-calling. I could shout out, "Big truck ten, right side wide." The only word that mattered was "truck" and meant to run the pick-and-roll.

I even planned to yell out some plays just to confuse and, I will admit, annoy Darren.

I would work in the names of famous Lakers players, which was sure to get Darren's attention, while I called plays. Stuff like "The Big Dog, James Worthy," or maybe "Magic Johnson in a rocket." It was going to make Darren nuts that I was using plays named after his favourite players.

I could hardly wait.

The night before the big game, we turned our cabin into a practice facility. We pushed all the bunk beds against the walls and hung my laundry bag on the door as our basket. We didn't have a ball, so we passed around one of my basketball shoes. I'd call the play, five of the campers would walk through where they would move, and the last guy to get passed the "ball" would drop it in the "basket." Then we would switch players and run another play. As this bizarre little practice went on, I started calling trickier plays. "Pat Riley in a go-kart with a full-tilt boogie." But the guys were so prepared, they executed everything perfectly. Eventually, I let the guys start calling their own plays, and they did pretty well. Most of the time, they just changed one thing about a play I had called earlier. If I said "Baby monkey 17," they would call out, "Baby uh-gorilla 17," just a few minutes later. Then, before long, one of the campers, I think it was Tony V. but it might have been Tony C., realized they could get a laugh out of the other guys with a rude play call. It was something like, "Let's run, your team plays like crap, which is brown," which got a lot of laughs. That was followed up with, "I peed in your water bottles, that's why it's yellow." That got even more laughs. Then someone shouted, "I got a play for you, *that Italian word*," and the guys in my cabin were hysterical.

I'll be honest. I laughed too.

It was a funny line delivered at the exact right moment.

Since it was not directed at anyone and we were safe in the confines of our cabin, I let it slide.

No harm, no foul.

The whole cabin was roaring with laughter. I knew it was time to end the practice and call it a night. The campers went to bed giggling about the last play call, and I fell asleep confident. Which was good, because the next day turned out to be a much bigger game than expected.

Because of the timing of the "cabin challenge," we had a huge crowd. Not only had most of the families of the campers come for family weekend, but most of them were very large families, and since our game was during the last "spare" of the evening, lots of the other cabins and their families had dropped by to watch.

The small bleachers beside the court were filled with parents, brothers, sisters, uncles, and aunts, and even a couple of very old nonnas (one of the very few Italian words I learned). The grassy hill on the other side of the court was filled up with camp counsellors, CITs, and campers from other cabins. This group included the counsellor that Darren was dating, and the counsellor that I liked but had been too nervous to say much more than "hello" to for the entire summer.

This was not going to be just a regular game.

Before the game started, I told them the first play we were going to run, a simple pick-and-roll, "Mad Dog 9."

We won the tip-off. I brought the ball down the court.

Darren waited for me just past half-court.

I shouted out the name of the play to remind my team. "Mad Dog 9" didn't work.

Neither did "Big Boat Left."

"Purple Rain" was a bust.

So was "Snake in the Grass."

Before I even had a chance to taunt Darren by calling the "Kareem Abdul-Jabbar rides a tricycle" play, we were losing by eight points. I did what any good coach would do.

I called a time-out. I tried to get them to calm down, reminded them to keep moving, smiled, and sent them out to try and execute "Monster Truck."

It didn't work either.

Nothing did.

Every pass got intercepted.

Every rebound went to them.

Every shot they took went in.

Every shot we took didn't.

To make it worse, they didn't even call any plays; they were just making it up as they went along. But that wasn't the worst part. The worst part was when Darren asked me, "Do you guys really have plays, or do you just like calling out random words?"

That one hurt.

I'll admit, I wasn't thinking clearly. I was tired and frustrated, and maybe I was suffering from a bruised ego, but when I did what I did, I was not thinking clearly.

I was inbounding the ball, trying to think of a play to call. I had run out of colours and animals and modes of transportation. Then I remembered the practice in our cabin with the laundry bag and the shoe. So I yelled out, "I got a play for you, *that Italian word*."

I threw the ball in.

There were two dribbles, a quick pass, then an easy bucket.

We scored for the first time in the game.

I ran back to play defence, smiling and laughing.

I didn't notice I was the only one laughing.

Darren missed his shot. I grabbed the rebound and led my team down the court. Now, I could have called another play. But the last play had worked, so I stuck with it. I yelled out, "One more time! *That Italian word.*" I remember hearing parents in the crowd laughing, mostly the Italian parents.

The ball went in the basket.

So I did it again.

This time down the court, one of my campers had the ball, so I shouted, "Hey, you better run *that Italian word*, it's the best play we got." More laughs, some really big laughs from the dads. A few harsh frowns from the nonnas.

My team was getting hot, so I called that play every time down the court. In between plays and later from the bench, I shouted stuff like, "Next year we're getting *that Italian word* written on our jerseys!" and "We should change the name of this camp to 'Camp *that Italian word.*'"

I thought what I was doing was harmless. After all, very few people in the crowd knew the meaning of the word. But without me knowing, the definition was spreading around the audience. Apparently, the kids who knew what the word meant had whispered it to the kids in their cabins, and very quickly everyone, on and off the court, knew what I was saying.

Except me.

But I was having a great time.

We couldn't miss.

We had tied up the game and it was all due to *that Italian word*. Not content to just keep using it when play-calling, I was encouraging the kids in my cabin to say it when they scored. I was shouting it when the ball was in the air, pumping my hands and chanting it while I ran down the court.

My team took the lead, and I started saying it even more, encouraging kids in the audience to join in. I led them in a sing-a-long of the Italian profanity.

"I say that Italian, you say word. That Italian … word!"

I even spelled it out:

"Give me a t! T

"Give me an h! H

"Give me an a! A

"Give me a t! T"

You get the idea.

The crowd was divided into three groups: people who were laughing because I was a clueless idiot. People who were laughing because I was embarrassing myself in front of the entire camp. And nonnas who crossed themselves and muttered in Italian every time I opened my mouth.

Eventually, the dinner bell rang and the game ended. Cabin seven, my cabin, the Italian cabin, had won. We lined up to shake hands with Darren's team, and when I got to the end of the line-up, one of my campers' dad was waiting for me.

He wrapped a big left arm around me, patted my chest twice, so hard he almost knocked the wind out of me, and said, "I know you don't know what that word means, so don't worry about it. It's not even that bad. But it's one that we don't say in front of the kids. We don't say in front of their mothers, and we especially don't say in front of their grandmothers." Then he laughed. It was a big laugh and one that told me he was in the group of people who were laughing because I was embarrassing myself on the biggest stage available to me. I realized what I had done, or not really. I still didn't know what the word meant, but in a sudden flash, I understood the weight of what I had said.

Over and over again.

Loudly.

In a numerous different ways.

As I waved from centre court to the girl I liked.

As I danced on the sidelines.

In front of impressionable children, their parents, and their nonnas.

I was a being laughed at and didn't notice. Until just now.

As the crowd moved from the basketball court to the dining hall, my eyes darted from group to group. I could see that every conversation was about me and *that Italian word*.

Uncles and aunts were recreating my most embarrassing moments from the game as they walked. Campers who had witnessed the game were running to tell the kids that had missed it. In the distance, some of the other counsellors were trying to gently break the news to the two head counsellors about what had just happened.

The camper's dad, yes, still laughing, helped his aged mother up from the bleachers and handed her both of her canes. As she began to take slow, shuffling steps toward me, he quickly stepped back to me and said, "Eh, if my mom starts to hit you, don't move, don't say anything. Just let her hit you. She won't do it for long, and at her age she won't hit you very hard."

Dread washed over me as he turned to join the others headed for the dining hall.

But I had to ask.

I had just made a huge mistake.

In front of the entire camp.

In a role that meant everything to me.

But I needed to know exactly what I had done, exactly what I had said. I asked what the word meant.

He just walked away, still laughing.

OUR SECRET
FISHING SPOT

WIFE AND KIDS ARE STILL asleep. I'm out the door before the sun is up. I grab my fishing gear and head out the back door of our house, careful not to wake anyone up. It's early, very early, too early. Too early in the day, too early in the year. But I need to go fishing. After a very long winter and a very late spring, I need to go fishing. Fresh air, relaxation, peace, and quiet. I need this.

I have to keep quiet, so I leave the lights off. I'm stumbling in the darkness as I gather what I need and head out the back door. Walking slowly toward the river, I leave behind our landscaped backyard, and the area beyond is slowly filled in with trees as I move away from the house. Soon I'm past the fort I built with the boys last summer.

It's a good fort with a drawbridge-style door and a dragon painted on the side. The fort marks the farthest from the house they are allowed to go.

It can be dangerous back here. There are no bears or wolves or poison ivy. But the woods are big enough they could get lost. Mostly, I'm concerned about the water. There's a large river that cuts along the back boundary of the property. I've checked the maps and traced it back a short distance to its source, a large freshwater lake. I guess it would be called "Falcon River," since that's the lake it comes from, but as far as I know the river has never had a name. Being so close to a large lake means the river is deep, wide, and has a swift current. All those things make it very dangerous but excellent for fishing.

That's one of the three things that make it such a special spot. First, it is excellent for fish. The topography of the river is exactly what anglers look for in a fishing spot. Upriver, there is a large area of shallow water that runs very fast over some large rocks sticking out of the stream. This is known as the Riffle. It is perfect for young growing fish. Lots of places to hide and plenty to eat.

After that is a large area of deeper, cooler water that moves much slower. This is known as the Run. It's where juvenile and adolescent fish like to live. Larger things to feed on, and they can find a home in the gentle current.

Then there is a quick bend in the river. There the water forms a deep, dark, cold well where the current can barely be seen. This is known as the Pool. This is where adult fish like to live and grow. Lots of large things to eat and plenty of deep water to grow really large.

Here is our secret fishing spot.

This Riffle-Run-Pool pattern is every angler's dream, but only my family ever fishes here.

That's the second reason it is special: it's hidden from everyone else.

Not like a Narnia thing, with a secret entrance or where you have to know the elvish password to open a magic door. Anyone could walk to the river and find our secret fishing spot, but no one ever has. In part, it's due to the shallow Riffle portion upriver. No boats could make it through there, and if they decided to portage, they would most likely pass right by the Run and Pool portions without ever knowing they were there.

If the big rocks of the Riffle stopped them and they carried their canoes on the far side of the river, they would find a large hill along the river's edge. Running for about a thousand paces, which is a lot when you are carrying a canoe, the hill has a steep bank on the land side and a sheer drop on the river side. Plus the hill is covered in low, thorny bushes and crowded by young trees. Even if the explorers put down their canoe and climbed the hill, they would find the thorns a hassle, and if they did reach the top, there would be no way to climb down to the water.

If these paddlers got out on my family's side of the river, they would never see the Pool. That side is hidden by a tight grove of trees that encircles the Pool. The large trees on the water's edge have fallen inward as the soft shore struggles with the immense weight of the huge trees. They create an umbrella effect that hides the riverbank so well, almost no sunlight makes it through.

The smaller trees surrounding them have fallen and sprouted at odd angles to create a ground-level barricade around our secret fishing spot. To get through, a person would first need to know where to look, then they would have to crawl under a certain fallen tree. Its trunk is huge, too big to move or climb over. But underneath, there is a small space where water has washed away the soil, leaving a narrow ditch. That's the entrance. Nothing magical. Just a dirty ditch barely big enough to crawl through.

No one would do that unless they knew what was on the other side, and no one outside of my family knew about it. It was my grandfather that showed it to me. That's the third thing that makes it special: my grandfather.

He is always there. Rain or shine, from as soon the ice melts to when the kids go back to school. It doesn't matter how early in the season it is. If the ice is gone, he'll be there waiting for me.

One time I was here so early in the season that I could still see my breath. It was when my childhood friend James had passed away. I thought I wanted to be alone. The air was so cold, I had to have one hand on the rod and the other buried in my pocket to stay warm. Even then, my grandfather was already there.

It didn't matter what time of day. Another time, I came out there so early, I had to carry a flashlight. It was closer to night than day, but he was there, waiting for me. The sun was only just creeping over the craggy hill on the other side of the river, but he was there. We talked about the scandal at the church. I asked whether I should keep going, find a different one, or give up church altogether.

We talked for a long time that morning. I can't remember if we caught anything or even fished. But I was so glad he was there waiting for me.

When I make it to that certain fallen tree, I put my rod and tackle box down in the ditch. Not really a tackle box, it's an old metal toolbox my grandfather gave me one summer a long time ago. I had looked at bigger, nicer ones in the store lots of times, but the one he gave me was perfect.

I have to crawl and push my gear through before me. When my grandfather took me here the first time, I was small enough that I only needed to duck my head to fit underneath. Now it is much tougher. I am certainly bigger, and my knees and back hurt just looking at the low opening.

I pass under the tree, shoving my gear along, and wonder what I would do if he wasn't there. But of course, he's already waiting for me.

I knew as soon as I heard it. The soft swish of the fly line.

It is barely audible, not much louder than the distant trickle of the water over rocks. But I can hear it.

He looks just like he always did: brown hip waders and a wide-brimmed tan fishing hat ringed with home-made flies. A red plaid shirt that he was old enough to call a "Buffalo check" pattern. His rod is all one piece and made from ash. The line is light blue, and he would have spent hours last night rubbing it with candle wax to make it waterproof. The creel on his hip was a hand-me-down from his father. It belongs in an antique shop. It's a wicker basket that sits flat on his hip; it's where he keeps his catch, as well as a sandwich that his wife has wrapped in wax paper, two if he's going to be fishing with his grandson. I smiled at the idea of there being a bologna sandwich in there for me.

He smiles at me and then turns his attention back to the water. I set the old green toolbox down on a log and flip the latch open.

In my rush to get down here, in my need to get down here, I forgot to pick up live bait. The lures will have to do. They have a light grey underbelly with a light brown back covered in dark splotches. They are designed to look like a baby trout, known as parr. I stare at it for a while in my hand. I think about the fact that a trout's favourite food is young trout. I think about the cheap piece of rubber designed to look like that. I think about the fact that it will never decompose. If it fell off my hook, it would sit at the bottom of the river forever. My grandfather is using lures too, but not rubber ones from the store. He ties his own flies with scraps from my grandmother's sewing kit.

I tied the lure on with a "Davy" knot. Grandfather taught me how to do that too. Every time we were fishing, he'd tell me that he knew the guy who invented that knot. Young enough to believe anything and be impressed by everything, I'd say, "Really, Grandfather?"

He'd say, "Sure, I knew him. We were in the war together. One time we got shelled when he was in the shower. He jumped into a foxhole with me with nothing on but a helmet and one boot." Then we'd both laugh.

Each time it was a different story about how he knew "Davy" in the war. It was probably a different army buddy each time I heard about "Davy," but to me, it was one guy who was in a lot of very funny stories.

I remember growing up thinking about how fun it must have been to go to war. According to the stories my grandfather told me, going to war was a lot like summer camp. The beds weren't good, the food was terrible, and you missed your family, but you came home with lots of fun stories about all the friends you made.

I don't know what to say, so I just start fishing. I cast my rubber lure and plastic bobber into the middle of the pool and wait in silence. He seems content to wait for me and continues the fluid and practiced motion of a fly fisherman.

From the soles of his feet to the top of his head, nothing moves except his arms. He is as still as a statue, but there is no tension.

In his left hand is the beginning of a huge loop of line. With this hand, he will carefully control the amount of line that he lets out, and he needs to be precise.

In his right hand, he holds the ancient rod. Ordered from a catalogue after he got home from the war, it probably cost him half a day's pay.

He swings the line toward the water, then pulls it back. It sails across the shore toward the cluster of trees that keeps us hidden. The end of the rod freezes, the line and fly trails behind about to finish the loop. The moment the fly is as far behind as the length of line will allow, he flicks the tip of the rod toward the water, and then it zips back the way it came. Flicking the tip of the rod back and forth over his head, the line forms a loop behind him and then a loop in front of him.

With each pass, the fly at the end of his line gets farther away from him. The expertise he has in his left hand means just the right amount of line is let out at the end of each loop. This is how the fly fisherman is able to cast exactly where he wants it. He builds momentum in the line until he has the fly moving at the exact speed needed to send his hook exactly where he wants it to land. When he lets go with his left hand, the loop in front of him unspools and the tiny lure at the end sails over most of the width of the pool and lands at the edge of a dark patch of water. The lure is tiny and weighs almost nothing, but is heavy enough to dip under the surface of the water and sink for a moment before floating back to the surface, just like a bug that has fallen into the water would do. He watches the floating wax-covered blue line for a sign that a trout has taken the bait.

I look from my plastic bobber to his blue line about a dozen feet away. I'm about to say something when he pulls his fly back with a snap. If a fish were going to bite, it would have happened by now, no point in waiting. Time to cast again.

I watch as his left hand pulls in the extra line and his right hand flicks the rod back again, beginning the process all over. Snap backward, build up momentum. Snap forward, build up momentum, let out some more line. Snap backward, build up momentum, let out some more line. His eyes are fixed on his target, and the fly lands exactly where he was looking, just a few feet downriver from his last cast.

"You know the reason why I'm aiming for that dark patch?" he asks. I shake my head, still a little unsure of what I'm doing here, feeling very much like a little kid here with my grandfather so many years ago. "It's 'cause of the log under the water," he says. "If you squint, you can just make it out. See, the fish sleep near there for safety. So this time of the day, they are just waking up, not really hungry just yet. I'm going to have to drop my lure right in front of their noses to get them to come out from under that log." He looks at me and cocks an eyebrow, hoping I will catch his meaning.

I've made a mistake, and he shows me my error, but he does it the way that someone who loves you does, without you knowing you are being told you are wrong.

I quickly reel in my line and recast. It lands almost exactly where I was aiming, just a few steps upriver from where his fly just landed. He smiles and withdraws his line to start another cast. "So how are you?" he asks.

"Good," I say as a reflex. "We're renovating the basement in the spring, adding some storage. The boys are doing well, good grades in school, we took the training wheels off their bikes, and they can really whip up and down the street now. Plus, we're booking a vacation, maybe rent a cottage next summer." I rattle off everything on my list and end with, "Yeah, good."

We're both silent as he casts again, and I tug my line a little against the current. After his fly hits the surface of the water, he turns his head to me ever so slightly and says, "I asked how *you* were doing."

"I'm good." I try to reinforce it by repeating it. "Yeah, I'm good."

He casts again. I know he will wait in silence all day if that's what it takes. I look down and focus on the knob that adjusts the tension on my reel.

"You look tired," he says, preparing for another cast.

"Yeah, I haven't been sleeping well," I say. That isn't the reason I wanted to talk, and he knows it. "It's just, well, I'm not sleeping," I say, looking down at that same knob. To be honest, I'm not even really sure what it does. "I just can't sleep. I'm tired. But I can't sleep. I spend all day exhausted, waiting for when it's finally time to go to bed. I get through all the things I have to do. You know, work, and the kids and the chores around the house, and when it finally is time for bed, the thing I've been waiting for all day, then I can't sleep."

He draws in his line again, a meditation in precision and practice. I keep talking. I didn't know how to start, but now that I have, I can't stop.

"Before I've even closed my eyes, I've started to worry about something small, like the car breaking down or something. Then before I can stop, I start to think of something a little bigger to worry about, like what happens if my wife gets sick, I mean really sick. And then my mind starts running on this loop where I'm thinking of bigger and bigger things to worry about. Before long my heart is racing, my chest hurts, and hours have gone by."

He casts again. He knows I'm not done, so he just waits. "I was actually handling it pretty well. I was." I honestly believe that, but I can't tell if he does. "But then something changed. I wasn't just thinking that bad things could happen. It started to feel like they already happened. Like, I went from lying in bed thinking, what if I get cancer, to thinking I *had* cancer. I was thinking that it would break my wife's heart, we'd lose the house, and the boys would grow up without me. I knew I didn't have cancer, but I'd wake up with the terrible feeling that I did. Every night I was finding something terrible to worry about and convincing myself that it had really happened …" I trail off before apologizing. "Sorry, this is stupid."

"Why is it stupid?" he's quick to ask, turning his head to look at me while still expertly drawing in the line with his left hand.

"I mean 'cause I'm worried about nothing. I'm inventing things to worry about," I say, cranking in my line just to have something to do. "You, you had things to worry about. You had *real* things to worry about. You immigrated here when you were, what, fourteen years old? Didn't have a penny to your name."

He interrupts for the very first time. "Yes, and I was worried for most of that time."

I adjust the lure a bit, hiding the hook a little better in the back of the rubber parr. "Sure, but what I'm saying is, like, you went off to war."

"I was worried most of that time too." This cast is a little farther out, getting dangerously close to getting his hook snagged on the sunken log.

"Yes, but you handled it. That's my point. You went off to war. You faced all that danger and death, and you were able to handle it. I can't handle being alone with my thoughts. I can't handle problems that are only in my imagination. I can't handle anything." I suddenly feel weak and embarrassed.

"Yes, maybe I did," he says, then takes a short pause. "But lots of men couldn't. Some people are just different."

"Weak," I reply in a murmur directed at the water.

"Not weak," he says, turning to face me for the first time, "just different." Then a long silence while he casts. And I think about those two words, over and over again: "just different." A bird breaks the silence when it thrusts out of the trees on the other side of the river. I watch it dart away in quick bursts of flapping.

Then a wave of exhaustion washes over me. I am suddenly and completely exhausted. Yes, it is early, and no, I didn't sleep well last night. But that's not it. My doctor says it is a coping mechanism. My brain is so emotionally overwhelmed that it tells my body to go to sleep. My brain is telling my body to shut down because it can't handle what's going on. She said that it is our mind's way to protect itself. We may not recognize it. It may not be the right way to handle the situation. But it happens. The mind takes care of itself in the only way it knows how: by telling the body that it is tired and needs sleep.

I know this is true. I knew it was true the first time she explained it to me. I know I'm not this tired; my body is fine. But I feel exhausted regardless. I'm thinking about lying down in the shade of the trees behind me. That happens a lot to me, at work or in my car at red lights. I have to fight to keep my eyes open. Every thought in my head is that if I go to sleep, when I wake up things will be different. I will feel different. I will *be* different.

He interrupts my spiralling thoughts by correcting my story. "I was fourteen. You got that part right. That was considered a grown-up back then. But when I came here I actually had one hundred dollars, a fortune back then." I squint at him in silent disbelief. I've heard the story from my father dozens of times. How his father came to this country "without a penny to his name, his new bride, and one steamer trunk that they carried between them." My dad always seemed proud of that idea. A pair of new immigrants, young and in love and heading to a new world with everything they owned in the world carried between them. Very romantic.

He recognizes the disbelief on my face. "It's true. The government wanted to attract farmers to move to the area, so they started a program. If you had one hundred dollars and a farming background, they would give you forty acres of farmland. So I borrowed fifty dollars from my father, asked your grandmother's father if I could marry her, then I asked him if I could borrow fifty dollars, then we moved here." He laughs quietly at the memory. I smile and look at the lines on his face.

Wrinkled, yes, and deeply, but soft. I have seen so many men his age that look hard and creased. He isn't fat but his skin is plump, a constant healthy glow and a permanent tan from all those years working in the sun on the family farm.

"I lied when I said I was a farmer," he continues. "Never been on a farm in my whole life, but I thought, how hard can it be to grow vegetables or milk a cow? Problem is they gave me an apple orchard." He casts again, forming a huge loop of line in the air, flicking the rod back and forth before firing the fly out over the water again.

He turns to smile at me and says, "For the record, growing apples is very hard." He nods and smoothly recalls the line with his left hand. "Especially that first year.

We had a cold snap, then not enough rain, then some trees got infected with flyspot. But we made it to harvest. Your grandmother and I picked the entire orchard by ourselves in those first few years. We were too poor to hire pickers back then. So, from sun-up to sundown, every day, we picked apples. This particular day, we'd been picking for weeks. Tired to the bone, the both of us. Just as the sun was setting, we're washing up behind the barn. We worked through lunch and hadn't had dinner yet.

"I'm looking down at the ground beneath the trees, and it is covered in rotten apples. They've ripened and fallen off the tree before we can pick them. By the next morning, the insects will have found them and they won't be any good to anyone. Nothing but waste. We've been breaking our backs to get our apples to market only to have half of them end up rotting on the ground." Another elegant cast before he continues.

"So I'm looking at the orchard floor, getting madder and madder about these rotting apples, when your grandmother asks what's got me frowning. I don't want to say what I'm thinking, so I just say, 'I tell you Abby, anybody came to this farm, they'd take one look at the ground and think we sold the worst apples in the world.' She smiles and looks up at me and says, 'Well, then they would be looking at the wrong place.' Then she pulls me close and turns me so I am looking back out at the orchard. Then she points up at the top of the closest tree. There the apples are so big and red. There they get the most sun, plus they are hard to get to, so they are never picked too soon. Then she says, 'When I look out there, all I can see are the best apples in the world.'

"Then she kissed me and headed inside to start supper."

Another cast, and the line forms the perfect loop in front and then behind us, then his lure sails over the water and lands exactly where he was aiming.

I reel my line in, tuck the hook under the bottom guide loop, and crank the line tight. Just like he taught me. I let out a deep breath. It makes me feel like I've holding it in for months, and I say, "Thanks."

He smiles at me with ruddy farmer's cheeks that lift up and almost make his eyes disappear. I close up my toolbox/ tackle box and head for the hidden opening that will force me to crawl back through the shrubs.

I need to say something more. I'm not really sure what, but I need him to know how much I needed to talk to him. How happy I was that he was here to listen.

"Thanks, Grandfather. I like fishing with you."

"Were you fishing?" he asks while deftly using his left hand to begin the process of reeling in his line. "One of us was fishing," he says, lifting an eyebrow. "I'm not sure what the other one was doing." I'm surprised by his humour. I remember my grandfather being lots of things, but funny was not one of them.

"You're right. Thanks for listening to me talk while you fished," I say, correcting myself.

"You might tell yourself that you need to go fishing." As he talks, he starts to wade into the river. His feet disappear as the water flows over them, then his ankles and then his calves as he steps in deeper and deeper. "But you only come fishing when you need someone to talk to, and I'm only here because you think no one else will want to listen, or maybe you think no one else will understand." The water is very quickly getting deep, almost to his waist, as he turns downstream and begins to cast to a new spot.

He's right, of course. I wanted to talk. But whenever anyone offers to listen I always say, "I'm fine, really, thanks."

When I need help, and someone offers it, I always say, "I'm just tired, that's all."

When I need someone to listen, I tell myself, "They have their own things to worry about. It's not right to burden them." So instead I come here to see him.

After my childhood friend died, I came here.

After the scandal at the church, I came here.

After his funeral, I came here.

That first time without him, I thought I wanted to go fishing as a tribute to him. Of course, I never expected to see him here when I arrived. But there he was, and he has been here every time I return to this spot. Every time I needed him to be here, he was here. Waiting for me at our secret fishing spot.

The trip back to the house is the same as it always has been. Same narrow ditch under the large fallen tree. Same shadows under the bushes and thorns covering the same tangles of vine. Same dirty puddles of mud that slick up the path back to the house.

But I don't look at any of those things.

I see green spring buds that have already crowned the tops of the trees. I see clouds bathed in soft yellows and oranges as a new day is starting. I see a house on a hill that has kept my children warm and safe every day of their lives. A house that has full cupboards and is often filled with friends. A house that contains all the people I love most in the world. And I keep my eyes on that all the way home.

CAMP POOP

I HAVE TO GO POOP.

Wha …?

I have to go poop.

So, wake up Dad. He can take you.

I tried.

So, wake up Mom. She can take you.

I tried.

You're going to have to wait until morning.

I *can't* wait!

I rolled over and pretended to go back to sleep. The cottage was cold, but inside my sleeping bag I was nice and toasty. I pulled the bag up to my ears. Then she started to cry. No tears yet, just that hitching breath little kids do when they are working their way up to sobbing. I might not have been the best big brother, but I wasn't about to leave her crying in the dark beside my bed.

Okay. Go grab the flashlight and I'll take you.

She stopped crying and let out a relieved sigh.

Don't bother putting on your shoes. Just put on Mom's sandals.

While my little sister headed to the front door of the cottage, I headed for Mom and Dad's room down the hall. I was still holding out hope that I would be able to wake one of them and they would have to take my little sister to the outhouse. I knew it wouldn't work before I even made it to their bedroom door. They were both snoring very loudly. I knew that they had stayed up very late playing cards with some of the other couples who had cottages nearby. It was pointless to try to wake them. They were both heavy sleepers. I had no choice but to take my little sister to the outhouse.

I resigned myself to the task and headed to the door where she was waiting. I grabbed my raincoat from the rack beside the door and got up on my tippy-toes to reach the latch that kept the front door closed. Then I stepped out on the front porch and waited for my sister.

Beyond very late, it was actually probably very early. I could have checked the clock on the wall of the cabin, but I was too young to read the hands on a clock very well.

It had been a hot summer day and a cool night, so a low layer of fog was lingering between the trees. It would burn off as soon as the sun was up, but for now it gave an eerie look to the forest floor. I had never seen any horror movies — again, I was very young, so I wasn't scared of monsters hiding in the mist. I just wanted to get back to my sleeping bag.

Come on.

Thanks for taking me.

It's nothing.

The walk wasn't that far. But it seemed a longer walk when, like me, you were sleeping just moments ago, or, like my little sister, you really had to poop.

Why did we have to walk to the outhouse? 'Cause our cottage didn't have a bathroom. Heck, it didn't even have running water. Heck, it wasn't really a cottage. My parents called it a "bunkie."

Just three rooms, two windows, and the electricity was an extension code that came in through a hole in the wall. For that reason, there could only ever be one thing plugged in at a time. You could make toast and you could listen to the radio, just not at the same time.

The outhouse was the only place around that had running water. Just off the main road, it was a small brick building with four tiny rooms: a men's bathroom, a women's bathroom, a men's shower, and a women's shower. Outside there was a bright silver tap for drinking water. All the families in the area would come there to fetch the drinking water for their "bunkies" or take their turn in the shower. Again, I didn't think it was a long way from our bunkie, but I wasn't the one who had to go.

Our bunkie was just temporary while my dad built the cottage. The idea was that we could spend a few weeks each summer staying in the bunkie and building our cottage. Then in a summer or two, when the cottage was finished, the bunkie would be used as a storage shed or maybe fixed up to be a guest cabin.

Of course, I didn't know it at the time, but the money for the land and the cottage had come from my grandfather when he passed. My mom's dad had left it to them in his will with the intention of them building something for the future. I'm told there was talk about starting a family business, but in the end my parents decided that my dad would build a cottage on some waterfront property in a place called Falcon Lake.

I say my dad built the cottage, but he had help. Dad was a carpenter, so he knew lots of people who worked in the trades, plumbers, electricians, that kind of stuff.

My dad also had a regular helper: me.

I was certainly too young to be doing this kind of thing. I had no idea what I was doing. I could barely lift some of the tools. I got tired very fast. I got bored even faster. But Dad insisted. He kept saying it would "make a man out of me." All I really understood was that my mom and sister got to enjoy their summer at the lake. I had to work.

I should say that I'm not mad at him. He was never mean, just a little out-of-date in his thinking. He used the phrase 'cause that's what his dad would have said to him. "It will make a man out of you."

I know what he was trying to do. He was very clear about what he wanted me to learn. But I was just a kid. I didn't understand. I couldn't understand.

I would have liked it more if I could have played in the lake with my mom and sister. Then maybe I could learn to be a man next summer. Or maybe he could get me a book from the library titled *How to Be a Man*. I was up for anything that didn't include climbing ladders, fetching tools, or carrying heavy lumber. It seemed to me that each lesson in being a man meant I got splinters in my hands.

I should probably explain that my dad wasn't into all that "alpha male" crap. He was a smart guy. He knew that stuff is nonsense, and he had called out the guys who worked with him whenever he heard that kind of stuff. Dad knew that wolves run in packs, and their strength was in the pack. I remember him saying that in the wild, the parents are in charge and the pack is just the extended family. The only time there was an alpha wolf was when they were in captivity, and that wasn't how wolves were meant to live. This wasn't about him thinking men were superior. This was about him wanting me to grow up to be a good person. He just didn't have the right words at the time.

That night (early morning), my sister and I walked in silence for a while. I remember having the feeling of the two of us being out of place in the forest. It was a time for owls and raccoons. A time when no humans were supposed to be out. Feeling like I wanted to break the silence; maybe to let the nocturnal animals that we knew we were trespassing, we chatted as we walked.

What do you think you'll do with Mom tomorrow?

We saw dragonflies at the dock today, she said we could try and catch some.

Lucky.

Do you think you'll have to work with Dad all day again?

Probably.

Why?

He says it will make a man out of me.

What does that mean?

I have no idea.

We chatted and walked around the bend as the dirt road gently turned right from our bunkie toward the outhouse, then up a gentle slope as the dirt road straightened out and merged with another dirt road from another cottage. If our bunkie had been located on one of those other dirt roads, I might have been worried about getting lost on the way to the outhouse. But our place was a straight shot from the outhouse. Leaving the shared bathroom, my family's cottage was the last one. It was the very farthest from the outhouse, something my mother would mention often when we walked that dirt road in the mornings.

So there was nothing to do but walk and talk. When we ran out of things to talk about, since I didn't like the silence of the forest, I decided to impress my little sister with what I had learned in school.

You remember the time we caught lightning bugs?

Yep.

Did you know that they are also called fireflies?

Really?

Yep, wanna know something else?

Sure.

Did you know that they aren't bugs?

Really?

And they aren't flies either.

Really?

Mrs. Casey says they are a kind of beetle.

I can't wait till I'm big enough to go to school.

By the time we made it to the outhouse, my little sister was almost sprinting. Actually more like speed-walking. Her back was clenched, and she wasn't bending her knees, for obvious reasons. I thought of it as "the trots trots," moving fast as you can move without relaxing too much. As soon as she ran into the girl's washroom, I realized we had a new problem.

I had to go too.

Not number two, but too.

As well. I mean.

I had to go number one.

You know what I mean.

But I couldn't leave her alone. See, the boy's washroom and shower were on the other side of the building from the girl's washroom and shower. If I went to the other side, even if I was quick, my little sister could come out of the washroom and I would be gone. If she came out and I wasn't there, she could get scared, or lost, or worse.

I couldn't use the girl's washroom after my little sister was done. First, it was the girl's washroom and boys weren't allowed. I wasn't sure why boys weren't allowed, but I knew they weren't.

Second, if I did use the forbidden bathroom, my little sister would be outside, alone and scared. I didn't know what to do, but I needed to think of something. I just stood there, wishing my dad were there. He'd know what to do. He always knew what to do. Which tool to use for which job. What job to do first. Which one to do last. Or when we should work in the rain, which was the worst.

For my dad, being a carpenter also meant being a part-time meteorologist. Understanding the weather meant he could plan his work better. If it was going to rain later in the day, he would start the job earlier to get as much done as he could before the storm. Pretty common for people working outside. They tend to understand and pay more attention to the weather than others.

Keep in mind that the weather never kept my dad from working. He'd work in rain or snow unless it made the jobsite dangerous. Even then, he would be working somewhere else. He would often say that there was always "inside" work to be done. If he wasn't quoting the next job or working on paperwork, there were always tools to clean, fix, or sharpen. Dad always looked at it as what was the best use of his time. Was it best for him to start early and get as much completed as he could? Or spend time taking care of his tools so that when he was at the jobsite he was working efficiently and safely?

My dad used to say we needed to "make hay while the sun shines." I didn't know what that meant, but I knew when he said it, it was going to be a long day.

So, each morning, sometimes before he had even had a cup of coffee, my dad would listen to the forecast on the radio. Then he would decide what we were going to do that day. That's what he said a man does.

A man leads. They make a decision based on the information available and lead accordingly.

That's why sometimes we'd start working on the cottage before the sun was even up. And sometimes we'd end the day sitting in the back of my dad's work truck, cleaning tools. The plastic shell that covered the bed of the truck was like a travelling office. He specifically picked one tall enough that he could sit in cross-legged and be out of the elements. To a carpenter on a jobsite, the covered back of their truck was where they sheltered from storms, ate their meals, and occasionally napped.

So, if the weather was bad, we would sit in the covered bed of the truck and talk. He'd do most of the talking. I was usually daydreaming about all the other things I'd rather be doing: riding my bike, swimming, fishing, really almost anything other than sitting in the back of my dad's truck. Often I was wondering about what my mom and sister were doing. I'd usually imagine them having hot chocolate and freshly baked cookies and playing my favourite board game (Battleship) while I was in a cramped bed cap that smelled of gasoline and rusty tools. That's often when my dad would decide to get into his "rules."

A man leads. They make a decision based on the information available and lead accordingly.

It was one of his favourites. He was a leader for his work crews. He was a leader on the jobsite, and he often tried to use that day's weather as an example of what he meant.

I had looked at the long-term forecast before we left.

Uh-huh.

Listened carefully to the radio this morning.

Uh-huh.

Had the tarps and our rain boots ready.

Uh-huh.

Then decided we would get an early start on the work to make the most of the good weather.

Uh-huh.

Are you listening to me?

Uh-huh.

Standing beside the outhouse, waiting for my sister, I didn't know what I was supposed to do. But I looked at the information available to me.

I couldn't leave while my little sister was in the bathroom.

I couldn't make her wait alone while I was in the bathroom.

So I made a decision: I peed on a tree.

If my mom had seen that, she would have been pretty upset. Every time my dad would do that, she'd get mad. If we were out for a hike, and he walked off the path and said something in man-code like "I need to see a man about a horse" (which makes no sense), my mom got mad. Not yelling. They never yelled. But she would tell him to walk to the outhouse.

If we girls have to walk all that way to the outhouse, then you do too!

But it's a long way.

I know!

But I did it anyway. I knew I wasn't supposed to.

They make a decision based on the information available and lead accordingly.

Both of us, very much relieved, started back.

How did you learn about fireflies?

Teacher told us.

Really?

Yep, read us a story too.

A whole day learning about fireflies! Wow

Not a whole day. Spent most of the day doing math.

Uh, math. I never want to go to school.

As we started walking back, I remember thinking that math class was better than working with my dad. But it wasn't all bad; we always got a swim in before supper, and sometimes we'd take a dip at lunch if it was really hot. I just was too young to understand. He wanted to share. His time, his knowledge, his skill. Overall, I think he did things the right way. He never asked me to do anything I wasn't capable of. He was pretty encouraging when the job went well. And he made a point of explaining the task and what he wanted me to learn.

For example, one time I was too scared to climb up the ladder and bring him a tool. When I started to cry, he climbed down and told me.

Men are not afraid.

Being afraid is letting fear tell you what to do.

He pointed out that the ladder was secure. It was in good shape, and there was nothing dangerous to land on in case I fell. He had taught me how to climb so that I always maintained three points of contact. I had no reason to worry about falling. He said it was okay to be scared. Everyone gets scared, but you should never let it keep you from doing what needs to be done.

That idea occurred to me as my little sister and I walked to the outhouse that night. As we left it, we left most of the light behind. The bright spotlight over the two washroom doors was comforting when we were standing outside the outhouse. But we left that security behind as we headed back. All we had was Dad's flashlight, and to me the path seemed much darker now that it was all we had.

I knew it was better for us to make noise; my dad had taught me that. When we first started coming to this lake, my mom was very worried about bears. My dad told us we were too noisy ever to be eaten by a bear.

Honey, you can't say that.

It's true, they talk a lot and they are very loud.

Now, your father doesn't mean that.

Yes I do, it's true.

Shush now. Don't listen to him, kids.

(laughing) Look, you've inherited lots of great things from your mother.

(pointing) Watch it, mister.

Including your strong voice and your ability to converse on any subject.

That's better.

The bears will hear you coming and head the other way.

He explained that bears, like all animals, want easy meals. They don't want to have to run fast or travel long distances for a meal if they don't have to. Every animal will choose the easy meal over the hard one.

Dad said to eat a thousand calories, a bear would have to spend an entire day eating berries. Or it could lick the inside of our ice cream tub from the garbage. It would get the same amount of calories in seconds. If a bear heard something moving in the woods, it would most likely investigate to see if it was an opportunity for an easy meal. But if a bear heard something loud, something making a lot of noise as it moved through the forest, the bear was most likely going to go in the opposite direction. Easy meals are usually very quiet, not loud.

I knew there were bears in the woods. I had never seen one, but they had left behind lots of evidence. Every time we saw some of this evidence, my dad would always say the same thing. "Does a bear poop in the woods? Apparently, yes!" They also got into our garbage a few times. Dad made no jokes then. He must have found it less funny when the bear ripped open the garbage cans to eat our scraps.

We walked like that for a while, chatting in hushed voices, the beam of the flashlight sweeping the dirt road in front of us. Then I saw it. Well, I saw something. Well, I didn't actually see it but I heard it. We both did. It was a bear. Or a raccoon. Maybe a squirrel. But it was a something.

It was to the left of the dirt road, so I turned the flashlight in its direction, and it moved again. Maybe it was moving away. Maybe it was getting ready to pounce. I couldn't tell. Whatever it was, whatever it was doing it was low to the ground and hidden by the darkness. It seemed like it was staying just far away enough to keep from being seen. I was scared.

My throat went dry, and my heart started to pound. I could hear the blood rushing through my ears. My knuckles started to hurt as I squeezed the handle of the flashlight tighter and tighter. I wanted to run, but I knew I couldn't do that. My little sister wouldn't be able to keep up. I couldn't leave her behind. I couldn't abandon her to the something lurking in the woods. I had no choice but to stand up to the bear. I had to use whatever I could to scare the raccoon away. I had to make sure, even if I was afraid, that the squirrel didn't hurt my little sister.

I was just a little kid. Wearing rubber boots and PJs, my only weapon was a borrowed flashlight. But luckily, I had inherited lots of great things from my mother, including her strong voice and ability to converse on any subject. So I started yelling. I didn't stop to think of what I was going to yell; there was no time. So I just yelled.

HEYYYYY.

When that breath ran out, I went to the words that seemed to naturally follow.

HEYYYY, BATTER BATTER BATTER BATTER.

I walked over to the edge of the dirt road where the something had been and began hitting the bushes in front of me with the flashlight.

HEYYYY, BATTER. HEYYYY, BATTER. HEYYYY, BATTER.

My heart was in my throat, and I had forgotten to inhale, so I was gasping for breath, but by my last BATTER I was sure that the something was gone, my little sister was safe, and we started off to the bunkie again.

We didn't walk very far before my sister started to shiver, and it was my fault. I had told her to wear Mom's sandals, but I didn't tell her to grab her coat; I should have. Actually, I should have grabbed her coat when I grabbed mine from the hook by the door. Now here we were, walking in the dark on a cool summer night. I had on my pyjamas, my rain boots, and a yellow raincoat. She was walking in a cotton nightgown, with one of the Care Bears on the tummy, wearing Mom's sandals.

Here, take my coat.

It's okay, it's not that far.

Take my coat. I'll be all right.

Thanks.

She immediately zipped up the front of the coat I had been wearing open. Then she flipped up the hood and put her hands deep in the pockets. She was colder than she was letting on. She was wearing her nightgown, I had thin pajamas, but at least they had long sleeves and covered my legs. Another advantage of being a boy: warmer pyjamas and peeing outside. However, in my parents' world, girls spent their summer catching dragonflies and swimming in the lake. Boys carried two-by-fours and fetched tools. Maybe it was a draw.

Just the day before, I had asked my dad why we had to be the ones to build the cabin. To be more accurate, I had whined about why we had to be the ones to build the cabin. I asked (whined) why girls got to spend the day swimming while boys spent the day working. It felt extremely unfair. It felt like the most unfair thing in the world. It felt like the most unfair thing that had ever happened to anyone. I was very young.

To my dad's credit, he didn't raise his voice. He smiled when he said, "*A man takes care of his family. He puts them before himself, every time.*"

He explained that building this cabin was him taking care of his family. He was going to build a place that was safe and comfortable and that was ours. He was going to build a place where maybe he and Mom would live when they were older, and then someday maybe I would come to stay at the cottage when I had kids.

Yeah, but why do I have to be here?

'Cause you are helping.

Yeah, but do I have to?

Yes, 'cause you are learning.

Okay.

Please hand me that pull saw.

Okay. Which one is that again?

Before long, my sister and I had made it past the gentle downhill slope and made the final turn to the bunkie. I could really feel the chill; I started rubbing the edges of my ears to fight the cold. If the bunkie had been much farther away, I would be the one shivering. But I had no choice but to give her my coat. It was what my dad would have done, because *"a man takes care of his family. He puts them before himself, every time."*

We reached the door of the bunkie, which opened with a squeak, and I heard my parents' rhythmic snoring as we returned the raincoat and footwear back to their proper places.

I zipped myself back into my sleeping bag and shivered. It was that wonderful sensation of warmth returning, like climbing out of a cold lake and into a beach towel, the summer sun strong enough to heat the sand and toast your towel while you swam.

My sister, undoubtedly feeling the same in her sleeping bag on the other side of the small room, whispered in the dark, Thanks for taking me.

It's nothing.

I drifted off, thinking about the walk. Peeing on the tree, shouting at the something in the forest, and giving my little sister my coat.

I thought about my father's lessons.

A man leads. He makes a decision based on the information available and acts accordingly.

Men are not afraid. Being afraid is letting fear tell you what to do.

A man takes care of his family. He puts them before himself, every time.

As I faded off to sleep, I wondered if I was ever going to learn what he was trying to teach me.

THE WOLDGER AND THE
GREAT FOREST

IN HIS RIGHT ARM, HE carried the limp body of a dead chicken. His other arm was gone, lost years ago, and now all that remained of the left arm was a gnarled, ragged stump. Tonight, it was covered by a rough tunic.

He approached the village slowly, cautious with each step. While the sun had long since set and it seemed there was no one around to see him, he worried just the same. The moon was full and bright, and it was essential that he not be seen. At least not until he was ready.

He had travelled a long way from the Great Forest and was confident that no one had seen him as he walked.

He knelt down behind a large hay bale that marked the imaginary line where the farmer's field ended and the village began and plotted his course into the village.

In front of him lay a sprawling collection of buildings. He was amazed at how it had grown so quickly. It was twice the size now as it was when he last visited a few years ago. Then again, a lot had changed in the past few years.

He saw cart tracks that seemed to lead in every direction. Each hill as far as he could see held a cluster of crude barns and squat homes covered with thatched roofs. In the centre of this mess were a tall church, a small military outpost, a large smithy where the blacksmiths worked, and then the place he was looking for. It was the only one that showed any signs of life so late at night. It was the tavern.

Candlelight beamed out of every window of the long, low building. Thick smoke wafted from the two chimneys on either end of the building and even from his hiding spot far away he could hear music coming from the tavern. His timing was perfect. He knew where he was going. Now he just needed to prepare before putting his plan into action.

First, he dropped the dead chicken and stepped on its head. Then, reaching down with his only hand, he grabbed the part of the neck that stuck out from under his foot and pulled. The soft soil of the farmer's field made pulling the head off harder than he had expected. When it came loose, it made the usual sharp crack and wet tearing sound that he had heard many times before, but there was less blood than usual. He had not expected that. He paused for the briefest of moments, looking at the headless chicken in his hand before smirking. Only then did he realize that every other time he had done this, the chicken had been alive.

This time, since there was no beating heart, there was no splattering of blood. Since the chicken's heart had stopped beating long ago, he would need to use gravity to execute this part of his plan.

He held the headless chicken upside down and over his left shoulder. It hung for a second over the stump that was now all that remained of his arm, then the blood began to trickle out. When the left side of his tunic was wet with blood, he tucked the chicken (and its unattached head) deep into the hay bale to hide it. Then, just one more thing to do before he headed into the village. The man dropped down to his hands and knees in the field and started to crawl.

He only crawled a few feet toward the village, but that was more than enough. When he stood up, wet grass and thick gobs of earth stuck to his toes and his knees and his hands. As he walked toward the tavern, he rubbed his muddy hand on his chest and face and ran his fingers through his thick black hair to make sure there was at least a little dirt on every part of his body.

He kept to the shadows and made it unseen to the door of the tavern. He listened to the voices inside and knew he had picked the right place. These were farmers and labourers, talking about the struggles of the day and drinking while they wished for better days to come. He knew to wait for the fiddlers to finish playing before entering. As the last note of the song faded, he threw himself against the door, and when it burst open he fell to the floor of the tavern, screaming, "MONSTER!"

A crowd gathered around him. His bloody left side was pinned beneath him, his right arm extended and pointing at the door while he continued to shout over and over again, "Monster! Monster! Monster!"

A few of the older men knelt down to try to calm him while some of the younger men ran out through the door he kept pointing at. Their faces and fists were ready for a fight. One of the older men brought over a crude wooden stool and told the others to get the stranger up off the floor. Another gently pulled at his right hand to roll him over onto his back. When the one-armed man rolled over, the crowd got its first good look at the blood-covered tunic. The circle around the man on the floor suddenly got a little larger as everyone stepped back at the sight of the blood. The man on the floor could hear someone directly to his left retching. His plan was already starting to work.

He let one of the older men help him onto the stool as the group of young men burst back into the room. Out of breath, they each gave parts of their report to the hushed crowd: "ran all the way to the church but didn't see anything"; "no sign of whatever it was"; and "it must have heard us coming and run off."

The old man who had given him the stool brought him a ladle filled with cold water. "Here, drink this slowly," he said. The bloodied man thanked him and sipped at the ladle, sure to spill a little for effect. The kind man waited for him to hand back the empty ladle and then asked, "Who are you, stranger? What happened to you?"

The man on the stool took a long, deep inhale, letting the crowd's anticipation build, then replied, "I am a merchant, travelling here from the great city of the king. To save time, I decided to travel through the Great Forest instead of using the road that goes around it. I got lost and walked for days before I found a clearing. It was a long strip of clear-cut forest that seemed to lead right to this village …"

One of the young men at the door interjected, "Aye, that would be the road we are building. The king is paying us to make a road through the Great Forest."

An old man who was sitting just inside the door of the tavern, older than most, drunker than most, responded loud enough for everyone to hear, "Oh, he's paying us, is he? That's a surprise to me. I've been breaking my back for weeks and have yet to see any copper." The man went back to his drink while many of the men mumbled in agreement.

The stranger on the stool went back to his tale. "Glad to have finally found my way out of the Great Forest, but exhausted, I decided to rest for the night and built a fire. Sometime during the night, the fire died down, and I awoke to find more fuel, and that's when I saw the eyes. Just outside the clearing, they were huge and glowed yellow in the darkness."

The very old and very drunk man stood up from his table and said the words that the stranger was hoping to hear: "It's the Woldger!" Many in the crowd nodded, but it seemed to the stranger that they were afraid to say the strange name out loud. The old drunk remained standing but leaned heavily on the table.

Another man, sitting alone on the other end of the tavern, stood and shouted at the old man. "Sit down, ya old drunk. Before someone does us all a favour and takes away your cup." He then shot an angry gaze at the fat bartender, who pretended not to see him.

The large and angry man was dressed better than most of the others in the room. With clean, finely tailored clothes, he gave off a sense of authority, and he knew it.

Obviously intimidated, the old drunk shrank back into his seat. But the stranger wanted him, needed him, to be heard.

"Wait … what did you call it?" He pointed at the old drunk. "The Woldger? Tell me about this beast."

The old drunk peeked to his right, confirmed that the angry man was still looking at him, and spoke, only much quieter this time. "'Tis like a great wolf, only bigger. Bigger than any man. With powerful jaws and razor-sharp claws." His eyes scanning the room, he seemed surprised to have everyone's attention. He spoke a little louder, "Legend tells of a cursed man long ago who made a deal with the devil. He wished to live forever, but he was cursed to live on as the monster you saw. If the sun ever comes up and the Woldger has not fed, the deal for immortality will end and the man's soul will be condemned to hell. That was the devil's deal. The Woldger needs fresh blood every night in order to avoid an eternity in Hades. It must live forever as a blood-sucking monster."

"Sit down!" shouted the well-dressed man again, but this time louder and meaner. Slowly, the old drunk sat back down. The well-dressed man spoke with an air of authority, and the one-armed stranger rightly assumed he was the foreman of the planned road through the Great Forest. When the foreman was satisfied that he had heard the last from the old drunk, he turned to look at the stranger, but it was clear he was addressing everyone.

"It's an old wives' tale, meant to scare children into being good. There is no such thing as the Woldger. There is nothing in those woods except the beginnings of a road." He punctuated his last sentence by sweeping a pointed finger over everyone's heads. "A road that will be finished on time!"

The stranger knew he could not afford to let this man intimidate the crowd. He needed them on his side. He stood slowly, making sure that everyone around saw him hold on to the table beside him for balance. He spoke quietly, weakly. The men on the far side of the tavern leaned in. "Well, I do not know what this thing was called, but I do know what it looked like ... and I know what it did," he said, giving a glance at his bloodied left side where an arm once was. "It was huge, I can tell you that. If it was a wolf, it was the biggest wolf that ever walked this earth. Even on all fours, it was huge. I am no small man, and even though I was standing, I had to look up to see its eyes."

He pointed to the old drunk, looking for confirmation of his description. But the scared old man only glanced up briefly from his cup, never raising his head. "They were yellow eyes, pale, tired, lifeless eyes in the darkness. I thought I would chase it away with a rock or a stick, but when I bent down, it attacked. It burst from the shadows and lunged at me."

The stranger began to pace the room. He moved away from the door, walking backwards to the bar, where the fat innkeeper stood holding a cup of ale he had forgotten to bring to a customer. The barman, like everyone else in the tavern, was staring at the stranger with eyes wide and mouth open.

As he continued his tale, he paced around the room and watched as the audience followed him with their eyes. Some even shifted their chairs to make sure they could see the stranger as he moved. He had their attention. Now he needed to tell them his story; he needed them to believe it.

"It didn't run. There were no footsteps. In one giant leap it sprang out of the shadows, arms extended, long arms that could have hugged an oak. Each giant paw was tipped with talons like a black eagle. I could see rows and rows of sharp teeth in its foul jaws. Each huge tooth in its massive mouth seemed to shine, wet and slick with venom. I could see the sickly green film that coated its forked tongue and left bubbles of foam in between its fangs and in the corners of its mouth.

"It moved like a demon freed from the gates of Hell. It was flying right at me, a monster of matted fur, black claws, and venom-covered teeth.

"I had no time to run, or scream, or even beg for mercy. All I could do was raise my arm to try to shield myself."

By this time, the stranger had made his way halfway around the room. He passed in front of a fiddler who sat in shocked silence, still holding his instrument under his chin, frozen as he had been since the stranger burst into the tavern.

Before continuing, the one-armed stranger purposefully turned his bloodied left side toward the crowd. Some men, so wrapped up in his story, had forgotten about the injury and looked away when they saw the blood crusting and turning brown on his left side.

"It cut through my arm with a terrible snap!" the stranger shouted and slammed his hand down on the table in front of him, making the men sitting there jump. "With the ease of a sickle through straw, its teeth went through my left arm. Like the bow of a ship cutting a wave, my arm was gone. I fell onto my back beside the fire. My severed arm was on the ground beside me, and in between us was the demon. Lying on my back, it looked too big to be real, yes, very much like a wolf but too huge and awful to be any creature in nature. I whispered a quick prayer, since I believed I was about to die. I thought — no, I knew I was about to bleed to death in the woods. But then I saw the hunger in its yellow eyes and knew what was going to happen. I was going to die in the jaws of the demon."

No one breathed. No one moved. The crowd just stared in slack-jawed wonder as the stranger talked.

"I tried to crawl away from the beast, then the burning started. It felt like my blood was starting to boil, like I had crawled into my campfire. It felt like red-hot pokers had been stuffed into what was left of my shoulder. I lay back in the dirt and screamed as pain consumed me. The pain was so terrible, I began to hope that the beast would finish me and end my torture."

The stranger paused dramatically, then bellowed, "But then I decided, if I was going to die, I was going give the beast a scar or two to remember me by!" Most of the men cheered and banged their cups on the crude wooden tables that lined the room.

The stranger touched the bloody stump of his left arm with his remaining hand and winced dramatically before he continued. "I opened my eyes to see the monster with my severed arm in its mouth, gnawing, slurping, and sucking on the limb as my blood stained its black lips red. Suddenly, the burning stopped, and I could no longer feel the wound that was my left arm. Nothing. No pain, no burning, and the bleeding had stopped. It was then I realized the secret to the beast's hunger. It lived on blood. Not flesh. Blood. Its venom had sealed my wounds, preserving the blood in my body. To my horror, I realized that the beast wanted me alive. It wanted my blood. I was a fish cured with salt so I could be consumed at a later time."

Every eye in the room watched as the stranger completed his slow trip around the room and lowered himself slowly onto the stool he had been offered when he was helped up off the floor.

He sat, shaking his head slowly as if too scared to continue. Secretly, he was wondering if they understood. Did they realize he was describing a fate worse than death? He decided he needed to make sure. This was too important.

When he spoke again, his eyes were fixed on a small spot on the floor. "Don't you see? The Woldger doesn't just kill you. It's not a bear or a lion. It doesn't just attack and eat. It's filling its larder. It's planning its meals. It incapacitates you and takes you back to some awful lair where it feeds on you until there is nothing left. This is no hungry animal; this is a blood-sucking monster."

The stranger pointed to the old drunk, the one who had first said the words "the Woldger," and said, "You were right. This is a cursed creature. It does need blood every night, and it plans to live forever by draining us all. One by one. Drop by drop. There is no avoiding it; there is no fighting it. Every person who goes into the Great Forest will suffer."

The stranger was spent. He closed his eyes and fell silent. He looked so frail and sat so still that some men in the tavern thought he had died right there on a stool.

Then the foreman spoke. His eyes were drawn into a narrow line. "How did you escape?"

The stranger didn't move or say a word. The man repeated himself, louder this time.

The stranger looked up at the man but did not answer. Not used to people not answering his questions, the foreman pressed on. "How did you get away? How did you make it here? How are you still alive?"

The foreman pointed a meaty hand at the stranger with the strange story. "How are you not trapped in the back of some dark cave?"

He began to shout his questions. "How did a one-armed man escape from a creature that never leaves anyone alive?" He walked over to the stranger and hovered over him. He spoke loudly enough for the whole room to hear, but he held his face just inches from the stranger's and bellowed, "Tell us, how did you escape?"

Slowly, the stranger raised his head to meet the foreman's gaze. Of course, he had been expecting this part. But he needed a break. A moment to gather his thoughts. This next part was crucial; he would need to be convincing. The stranger turned from the foreman to address the barkeep and said, "May I have a drink?"

The barkeep presented the stranger with a cup full of cool water. The stranger had wished for whiskey or beer, but in a raspy voice he thanked the man and continued his tale. "I was lucky."

The stranger stood slowly, never losing eye contact with his accuser as he repeated himself. "I was lucky. I was lucky it was only my arm. I was lucky that the Woldger's plan was to keep me alive. I was lucky I had dropped my pack near the fire."

Then he turned his back to the foreman and addressed the rest of the men. "There I was about to be dragged off to the monster's lair, where it was going to feast on my blood. I watched in terror while it drained the last drops of blood from my severed arm. It was then that I noticed its eyes. No longer pale yellow, they had turned deep red. Having gorged itself on blood, fulfilling its deal with the devil, its eyes now glowed crimson surrounded by fur as black as the darkest night. Then it dropped my arm and turned to me."

The foreman scoffed and headed back to his private table at the back of the room. He made a point of turning his back to the stranger, showing everyone that he was no longer listening to this unbelievable story.

The stranger stepped up on the stool he had been sitting on as he continued the story of his escape, ensuring that everyone could see and hear him. "The beast reared up to its full height, towering over me as it dropped my severed left arm to the ground. I could see the arm was as white as marble. The monster had drained every last drop. Then it started to approach."

He jumped down off the stool and pointed to one of the younger men near the door. There was fear in the young man's eyes, and that fear grew with each step as the stranger approached. "I was finished, and the monster knew it. Its toothy jaws opened as it stood over me. I could see each fang, rooted deep in black gums, as long as my finger and sharp as the executioner's axe. I could see my own blood in its mouth, mixed with its dark green venom. It pooled in the back of the Woldger's mouth as it began to growl down at me. A wet, low guttural sound, like it was trying to tell me I was doomed."

The stranger grabbed the scared young man by the front of his shirt and pulled him toward the middle of the room. "The beast started to drag me off into the woods. I was nothing in its monstrous paws. Like a child carrying a doll." The young man was used to demonstrate the next part of the tale.

"This is when I got lucky," the stranger continued. "As the monster dragged me across the clearing, it pulled me past my dying campfire." The much larger stranger violently shook the scared young man to demonstrate his rough handling by the lumbering monster. "That's when my hand fell on the end of a branch sticking out of the fire." He grabbed the terrified man's right arm and stuck it straight out to demonstrate to the crowd. "I jabbed the burning end of the stick into the monster's eye, and it howled in pain. It loosened its grip only long enough to strike me in the head." With that, the stranger pushed the terrified young man to the floor of the tavern. Then he pulled the arm of the prostrate man up into the air, saying, "Dazed, I struck again, jamming the burning stick back into its other eye. And that was when the Woldger made a mistake." He turned away, leaving the scared young man staring up from the floor. He did not move, eyes wide and mouth open.

"Blinded, the beast lost track of me and reached down, grabbing the first thing it could get its claws on: my pack. Finding it heavy and covered in rough cloth, the monster must have thought it had grabbed me by my tunic. It quickly dragged the pack behind it and disappeared into the darkness of the woods, leaving me alive and alone. I ran until I saw the lights of this tavern and knew I must warn you all about the dangers of entering the Great Forest. I want you to understand it was nothing but luck that saved me. I was lucky with my arm. I was lucky with the fire. I was lucky the monster mistook my pack for my corpse. I tell you now, I will never enter the Great Forest again."

His tale finished, the stranger stood in the middle of the crowded tavern, silently surveying the faces, looking for a sign that his plan had worked and they believed his story. Everything depended on them believing his story.

Most of the men were looking down at their cups or whispering quietly to those beside them. Then a new voice addressed the crowd. "Neither will I," said a man seated behind the stranger. He stood up and took a simple pipe out from between his teeth. His mouth was a flat line across his face. "I'll not be entering those woods again. There is better hunting in other woods, closer trees to be cut for winter wood, and better work than to build a road for some far-off tax collector."

The group of men seated at his table all stood up with the pipe-smoking man. They were his friends or maybe his sons, but either way they were following his lead. The stranger watched in silence as other men at other tables followed the smoking man's lead, standing in defiance.

At almost every table, men began to say that they would not enter the Great Forest, they would not work on the king's new road, and they didn't want to fall victim to the Woldger.

The murmur of dissent quickly spread around the room, and soon the men were shouting their pledges never to enter the Great Forest. The foreman stepped quickly into the middle of the room, bellowed, "Oi, enough!" and the room quieted.

He pointed at the man with the pipe who had first stood up to him. "You will enter the Great Forest, and you will enter it tomorrow. You will continue to work on that road, and not only because I said so, but because your king commands it." His eyes swept across the heads of the men in the tavern. Each of them, even the man with the pipe, was looking down or at something in a far corner of the tavern, anywhere but at the flashing angry eyes of the foreman.

There was a moment of silence before the stranger began to speak. Surprisingly, he came to the foreman's defence. "This man is correct. Your king has ordered the building of the road through the Great Forest, and you, as his loyal servants, are to follow the bidding of your king." With that the stranger bowed briefly in the direction of the foreman, who let a toothy smile slide across his face, surprised to find a supporter in the smooth-talking stranger.

The stranger moved back to the stool and the cup that had been offered to him and lifted the cup to his lips, saying with a suddenly casual air, "And in return, I am sure your fair and gracious king will protect his subjects as they build his road." Then he took a deep drink and let his words hang in the air.

It was of course the old man with the pipe that spoke first. "You are indeed a stranger in this village if you think our king would send a single soldier to protect us. The only time he has ever sent soldiers to our town was when our taxes were late. Let him send workers from his great city to build his road."

"Aye," shouted a man seated at the same table. "Let them break their backs. Let them be eaten by the Woldger."

A young man across the room smiled and shouted, "You know they have no workers there. It's a whole city filled with nothing but tax collectors." Most of the crowd laughed and toasted his jest.

A man wearing numerous animal pelts stood up and addressed the crowd for the first time. "And how does this road help me? I hunt the woods nearby. Yes, I will get my pelts to the great city faster, but it will also bring more hunters to our woods. That means less to hunt and less coin for my pelts."

A murmur swelled around the man as he took his seat, then the foreman raised his hands, a move meant to quiet the crowd. When the chatter continued, he tried to shout over the noise. "The king will send out a hunting party, and they will make the Great Forest safe. There is no need ..."

A young man near the tavern door shouted over him, "Weren't you listening? This thing cannot be killed."

Others began to yell as well. "There is a fate worse than death waiting in the Great Forest"; "I'll not be bled dry for a road I'll never use and a king I've never seen"; "If we go in those woods again, we'll only be making the beast stronger."

Angry at his defeat, the foreman cursed and stormed out the tavern. Cheers rang out when he slammed the wooden door behind him.

The stranger finished his cup and got up from his seat, hoping to leave unnoticed, when the old man with the pipe approached. "We are grateful for your visit, stranger. We are lucky to have heard your warning, and we will heed it. But we were wrong to ignore your wounds. I will send for the healers to come tend to you."

"No," said the stranger quickly; he could not risk having his "wound" examined. He continued to weave between tables of men and head for the door. "I am rested and better. I must leave now."

"Why now?" said the old man, pulling on the stranger's one remaining sleeve, trying to stop him from his exit. "You must stay. You must rest."

The stranger stopped and turned to face him. He needed to leave, but he also needed to make sure he did it without making the villagers suspicious. He had not considered this; he needed to think quickly. "I'll get no rest here. I'll not stay in the shadow of that forest. Not after what happened. I have kin in a town far away from the Great Forest. I will live there. Far from that cursed forest." Then he gave a short bow before heading to the door.

The pipe-smoking man nodded in understanding and sympathy as he watched the stranger leave. He returned to his table and joined the conversation about the Woldger, the king, and the road.

The stranger headed away from the direction of the Great Forest. He was fairly certain he was not being watched, but he couldn't risk it. He kept the forest at his back until he was far outside the village, sure that distance and darkness hid him, then he circled back. He skirted the edge of the village, sure to stay in the shadows until he was back behind the hay bale where he had hidden the body of the headless chicken. Glad to find it untouched, he retrieved it and turned toward the Great Forest.

He had walked a long time before reaching a small clearing deep in the forest, and the night was just about over when he saw them: piercing yellow eyes, three sets, low to the ground and approaching slowly.

When he knew that they were close enough to hear him, he spoke. "There must be mighty hunters in these woods. They have stayed downwind from their prey. They have stalked their prey to assess the risk, and they didn't reveal themselves until they were sure that their prey could not escape. It looks like I am caught." He smiled to himself. "I guess I'll just lie down and die." Then he sat down on the floor of the forest, threw his right hand over his heart, and lay back.

At that, three small animals scrambled into the clearing, all shouting at the same time, each one trying to talk over the other.

"Father!"

"You're back, we missed you."

"Mother said you wouldn't be back until morning. Did you bring us anything?"

Each looked like a small wolf cub, only their black fur was unlike that of any wolf. It had a darkness to it, a moonless midnight black that made the creatures almost invisible in the darkness. If they were still and in a shadow, only their yellow eyes could be seen.

The three cubs pounced on him, licking his face, pawing his chest and nuzzling their heads against his. He smiled and wrapped his right arm around each of them in turn before their questions began again.

"What was the village like?"

"Why did you have to leave us?"

And then of course, "Did you bring us anything?"

He laughed as he scratched one behind the ears, one under the chin, and one along its jaw. He knew where each liked to be scratched.

"Yes, of course I brought you something. You will find a tasty chicken hidden not too far back the way I came. Mind you, it is well hidden, so you will need to use all your senses to find it. Off you go now, go find it."

With his permission, they bounded out of the clearing, headed back the way he had come, noses down, ears pinned back, and yellow eyes wide.

He stood and smiled in the direction the three cubs were headed, then he worried about them going too far away, so he shouted, "It's not too far. Turn around if you get to that lake where the falcons nest."

He wondered if they could hear him and would listen. He had been a father long enough to know that children hearing and children listening were two different things.

He could hear them bounding through the undergrowth and shouting to the littlest one to keep up. They all had much to learn before they could hunt in the Great Forest alone.

Turning his attention to the trees to his right, he spoke into the darkness. "They are getting better. They still follow too close and walk too loud, but they are getting better."

With that, another animal stepped into the clearing, much less like a wolf than the three small ones. A body like a wolf, certainly, but it moved more like a large cat. With the grace of a flowing stream, it slipped through the tangle of trees, making no more noise than a falling leaf.

He smiled at her. Her grace. Her beauty. Her strength. They left him in speechless wonder every time he saw her. "Hello, my love," she said as she moved to his side. He wrapped his arm around her neck and rested his head against the side of hers, breathing the smell of the forest pines in her fur. Another thing he loved about her.

"What happened in the village? Did you stop them? Why do you smell like chicken blood?" she asked as soon as their embrace was done. She wanted answers and knew the cubs would return soon, and then the conversation would have to end.

"It went well, I think," he replied.

"What did you do? Will they be back?" she hissed. She wanted to scream the words. His answers were everything to her, but she knew shouting would make the cubs return, and she would have to wait even longer for the answers.

"I told them a story —" he began.

"You told them a story?" she interrupted. "I thought you were going to kill the ones building the road."

"That would only bring more villagers to the forest, most likely with weapons, maybe even soldiers. This way is better," he said calmly.

"Telling them a story is better? How?" she asked. She had always trusted him in their lives together. Especially when it came to humans. But this was too important, and she was worried.

"I told them a story about a powerful monster that lives in this forest. One that would torture them cruelly if they ever entered the Great Forest again," he said, smiling.

"Do you think they believed you? Believed you enough to stay out of our woods?" she asked.

"Yes, absolutely," he said, looking into her pale yellow eyes. "I was just hoping to scare them, enough to stop them or maybe just enough to slow them down. I hoped that they would remember what they had named me, so long ago."

"And did they?" she asked, panicked.

"Yes, they did. In fact, the name 'the Woldger' seems to have become a bit of a legend in the village, which actually helped with the story. They seem to think that we are immortal, and oh, I added that we can change the colour of our eyes."

She scowled at him, not sure if she could believe something so outrageous. He shrugged at the absurdity and continued. "Plus, they seem to dislike the building of the new road and seem to be unhappy with their king." He finally told her what she wanted and needed to hear. "Yes, I think it worked, and no, I do not think we will be seeing villagers in our woods again."

She let out a quiet breath. It made her feel like she had been holding her breath all night. "You know these humans better than me. You know better how they react and what they are capable of."

"Yes, I do." He smiled and pointed to where his left arm used to be. It had been a long time since he had lost his paw in that hunter's snare. A very long time. Lots had changed since then. He had healed, he had met her, and they had their cubs. Before he met her, he might have attacked the road workers, maybe even the village itself. But now he was different. She had changed him. *They* had changed him.

"That's exactly my point," she said. "When we met, you said the people of the village were violent, ignorant, and not to be trusted. Has that changed?"

"No, all those things are true." He held her again, stroking her fur, hoping to calm her with the movement of his hands. "They are not to be trusted, they have no idea about the world around them, and they relish violence in every part of their lives. But trust me when I say this, to a human, nothing is more powerful than a good story."

It was then they heard the cubs howling loudly, letting their parents know they had found their prize. With that, he began the painful process of changing out of his human form, but soon it was over and the pair was headed toward the excited cubs.

The sun began to rise, and they travelled as a pack, three cubs and a pair of parents, one with four paws and one with three, moving through the shadows of the forest.

Known to some as the Great Forest, known to them as home.

ACKNOWLEDGEMENTS

NOTHING MEANS MORE TO ME than the love and encouragement of my family. Without them, none of this would be possible. My wife, Sally, gives me courage and support. I hope she knows that she means everything to me. My son, Joseph, is a hardworking man, but at the end of the day he always finds the energy to listen to a new draft or celebrate a single sale. My middle child, River, is wonderfully creative. They have ideas so brilliant that I am often forced to pay them the ultimate compliment and claim those ideas as my own. My youngest is Maddy, whose enthusiasm and willingness to try anything is inspiring to me every day.

Many of us are lucky enough to have a family we are given and a family we choose. The family I chose is called The Butters. They are always supportive, encouraging, forgiving, and kind. Their willingness to make a really big deal about every one of my tiny successes only makes me love them more. Please keep it up.

The nice way to say it is that my first book was inauspicious. But Dundurn Press showed me faith and confidence that I have tried very hard to justify. I continually meet people in the industry who say, "Dundurn does it right; they are the best." I always reply that they do and they are.

Once again, these stories started with my brainstorming buddies Drew Kozub and John Titley. They are two of the best storytellers in the world. It is my honour to take their ideas and change them just enough so that they cannot sue me. Thanks for sharing your brilliance.

Thanks to The Tragically Hip. They will never know it, but the boys in the band were with me every step of the way. Not just playing in the background during the writing and editing, but inspiring and teaching as well. The Hip told me that it was okay to tell a common story from an uncommon point of view, that improv can be scary but can lead to wonderful places, and that, sadly, it can't be Nashville every night.

Finally, the best part of being a writer is being invited to read in schools (don't tell the publisher), and I have been lucky enough to visit hundreds of classrooms, from kindergartens to universities. A special credit is due to Heather and Lou at the Nickel City Literacy League, as well as an inspiring student who once asked, "Did you *really* write that, 'cause it was actually pretty good?!?"

ABOUT THE AUTHOR

JEREMY JOHN has been referred to as a raconteur and an anecdotist, as well as other big words that he only pretends to understand. He is the writer (he thinks the word "author" sounds pretentious, another big word he only pretends to understand) of three collections of short stories that he (and only he) refers to as The Incredible Poop Trilogy. He currently lives with his wife, kids, and dog (that he was told would never sleep in his bed and *always* sleeps in his bed!) in Sudbury, Ontario.

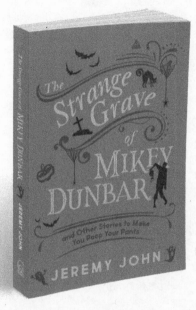

THE STRANGE GRAVE
OF MIKEY DUNBAR and
Other Stories to Make
You Poop Your Pants

Spooky short stories for the whole family that are perfect
for reading out loud on Halloween night, at a sleepover,
or around the campfire.